LET US
PREY

Also by
Monica Quill
NOT *A BLESSED THING!*

LET US PREY

A
SISTER MARY TERESA
MYSTERY
BY

Monica Quill

THE VANGUARD PRESS
New York

Copyright © 1982 by Monica Quill.
Published by Vanguard Press, Inc., 424 Madison Avenue, New York, N.Y. 10017-1194.
Published simultaneously in Canada.

Library of Congress Cataloging in Publication Data

———

Let us prey.
I. Title.
PS3563.A31166L4   813'.54   81-23072
ISBN 0-8149-0861-6   AACR2
Designed by Tom Torre Bevans.
Manufactured in the United States of America.
1 2 3 4 5 6 7 8 9 0

For Dorie and Bruce Saunders

One

There are two possible ways a child will react to the sight of Sister Mary Teresa in the full regalia of the Order of Martha and Mary, and Freddy was fascinated rather than terrified. He had wandered away from Joyce in the kitchen and now stood in the doorway of the study looking wide-eyed at the fat little nun behind the desk busy writing her daily quota of pages.

"Hi," Freddy said.

The scratching of the fountain pen went on. There was the sound of ticking from the large silver watch lying on the desk pad. Emtee Dempsey's starched winged headdress moved from left to right, like the carriage of a typewriter, her observations on the twelfth century emerging from the point of her pen in neat rows on unlined paper. Freddy entered the study and stood beside the nun.

Sister Mary Teresa, septuagenarian remnant of a once flourishing order in whose college west of the city she had taught history, now resident with Sisters Kimberly and Joyce in an old house on Walton Street — the three nuns all that remained of the M. & M.s — was absorbed in her work, Freddy was four years old and small for his age and, in any case, Emtee Dempsey's headdress cut off her peripheral vision.

"Hi," Freddy repeated, tugging at the old nun's sleeve.

Rosary beads clicked when Sister Mary Teresa turned, her gold-rimmed spectacles framing rounded eyes.

"Hello, young man."

"What are you doing?"

The trip from the twelfth to the twentieth century took a moment more. The nun put down her pen. Freddy reached for the watch and she let him take it.

"I am writing. What are you doing?"

He put the watch to his ear and concentrated on the rhythmic ticking as if it put him in contact with the formation of the Third Crusade, the fortunes of which were the topic of the chapter Emtee Dempsey was writing. Still listening to the watch, Freddy touched the huge beads of the rosary that hung from the cincture around Emtee Dempsey's ample waist.

"What is your name, boy?"

"Freddy."

"Ah. Has anyone ever told you of Frederick the Great?"

The nun scooped up the little boy and put him on her lap, pushing away from the desk. Her rosary and watch were one thing, the pages of her manuscript something else. She had frowned away Kim's suggestion that the manuscript be photocopied as it was written. Now, as she went on about the exploits of Freddy's namesake, the little boy still clamped her watch to his ear.

Looking on from the door of the study, Kim shook her head. "Sister, he doesn't understand a word you're saying."

"I am used to that. I taught classes of uncomprehending girls, among them yourself."

"He's four years old."

Freddy ignored Kim's entry, apparently content to sit on Emtee Dempsey's lap.

"Who is he?"

"A neighbor. Joyce agreed to look after him this afternoon."

"She is being delinquent."

"Freddy! Freddy, where are you?"

It was Joyce, calling from the kitchen. Kim went into the hall. "He's in here, Joyce."

Joyce, wearing jeans and a sweatshirt, an apron wrapped around her middle, opened her mouth in mock silent horror and hurried down the hall. She stopped when she saw her ward seated on Emtee Dempsey's lap.

"I don't believe it."

The old nun looked at her. "I find we have company."

"I'm sorry. I'm baking. He must have wandered away. Come on, Freddy, let's stuff ourselves with cookies."

The boy slid from Emtee Dempsey's lap, still clutching the watch. Joyce tried to take it from him but his grip tightened and he turned away.

"He'll tire of it," Emtee Dempsey said.

"I'll put a cookie in each hand and bring it back."

The watch had been presented to Sister Mary Teresa years before by her students on the occasion of the twenty-fifth anniversary of her entering the Order of Martha and Mary. Kim knew that it had great sentimental value for the old nun, not least because it recalled the college they had closed and sold. Emtee Dempsey had vowed to live her life according to the rule written by Blessed Abigail Keineswegs, foundress of the order. At the time she entered that would have seemed a very predictable future — convent life, classes, an orderly round of work and prayer, all her actions offered in service to the Lord. But the M. & M.s, as the Order of Martha and Mary was called, sometimes affectionately, had suffered more than most religious orders from the innovations of Vatican II. Nuns had left the order, new vocations dropped from rare to non-existent, feelings of guilt were expressed at the comfortable life lived on the ample grounds and in the pleasant buildings of the campus west of Chicago. When enrollment plummeted, fed on and feeding this sentiment, the place was sold and the proceeds distributed to the poor in a manner that had captivated the Chicago newspapers. Photographs of nuns in pants suits dispensing cash to the crowds pressing about them in the south-side ghetto adorned the pages of the *Tribune* and *Sun-Times*. More than enough money was kept to sustain the old house on Walton Street designed by Frank Lloyd Wright, gift of an affluent and grateful convert, and the sisters settled there to engage in more relevant work in the inner city. But attrition had continued and for some years now there had been only Sisters Mary Teresa, Kimberly, and Joyce. Emtee Dempsey, who had opposed the flashy switch to the social gospel from what she regarded as the more important apostolate of the intellect, felt her predictions were vindicated when the reformers eventually drifted out of the order.

"The college would have folded anyway," Kim would say when this sad history was rehearsed in sepulchral tones by Emtee Dempsey.

"There is no way we can know that."

"Surveys were taken."

Emtee Dempsey grumped. She was an historian of the old school who held that significant deeds are performed by heroic individuals against the odds. She was skeptical of statistical fatalism, alleged trends, or any view of human action that saw men as playthings of history rather than its agents.

"If the Apostles had been guided by surveys they would have gone back to their fishing boats."

"We were teaching only an elite."

"College students are always an elite."

"An economic elite."

"We had many girls on scholarships."

Kim had been one of them. Well, she never expected to win an argument with Emtee Dempsey anyway. What was the point? Kim had agreed with those who voted to exchange the Hanseatic habit designed by Blessed Abigail for ordinary clothing and she had favored the more direct apostolate to the poor. The trouble was that they had ended up with neither the old way nor an effective new way. Emtee Dempsey worked on her magnum opus on the Middle Ages, Joyce cooked and kept house, and Kim pursued her doctorate at Northwestern and acted as Emtee Dempsey's research assistant. The old nun did not like to leave the house, so it fell to Kim to check references at the library and bring home the books the old nun did not have in the collection lining the walls of her study. Slim, with pale red hair and a tendency to freckle, Kim wore a seersucker suit, the silver cross pinned to its lapel the only sign she was a nun. This sometimes led to embarrassments of a not unflattering kind. All the high hopes with which they had closed the college had come down to their odd existence in the house on Walton Street. Only Joyce moved easily among their neighbors. Hence Freddy's presence.

Kim put the books she had brought from the Newberry — Dr. Tedesco could not be more accommodating to his esteemed older colleague — on Emtee Dempsey's desk. The old nun grunted her gratitude. She drew her chair up to her desk and picked up her fountain pen. Kim felt dismissed.

When Kim went into the kitchen, Freddy was sitting on the little stepladder Joyce needed for the upper shelves of the high cupboards, a cookie in each hand, chocolate smeared on his face. Joyce stood in the back door, furtively smoking a cigarette, cupping it in her hand. Emtee Dempsey considered a smoking nun an abomination and Joyce deferred to this prejudice by sneaking her cigarettes. She pitched it outside and pulled the door shut.

"Where is Emtee's watch?"

Joyce crossed her eyes. "In his pocket. I'm going to have to wrestle him for it when his mother comes."

The sweet aroma of baking drove out the smell of cigarette smoke. The scene was even more domestic with Freddy chomping on cookies.

"Where did Freddy's mother go?"

"She didn't say."

"How long will he be here?"

Joyce shrugged. That was like her. Joyce was an easy mark for Freddy's mother and for other neighbors as well. She would not take money for baby-sitting their kids and more often than not washed dishes and cleaned house while she watched them. For a child to be brought to the Walton Street house was unusual. It was an odd thought that only Joyce, who had been neutral and indifferent when the order was torn by debate over its future, now served the poor and disadvantaged.

"How is she getting along with the father?" Joyce kept Kim informed on the ups and downs of their neighbors' lives.

"Enid is talking divorce. I don't really blame her. Besides, they weren't married in the Church."

"Are they Catholic?"

"She isn't. He should be. They had Freddy baptized. At least Enid said they did. Maybe she thought I wouldn't baby-sit for her if Freddy was a pagan."

"Can she support herself? She can't expect much from him, can she?"

"Who knows? He might pick the daily double at Arlington and live happily ever after."

Freddy, having eaten his cookies, fished Emtee Dempsey's watch from his pocket and held it in his sticky fingers. The poor little guy. Kim wondered what chance in life he had with his immature squabbling parents and a broken home in the offing. His mother seemed all too willing to leave him anywhere she could while she went off God knows where. Statistically, Freddy's future looked bleak. Kim would have liked to share Emtee Dempsey's distrust of statistics, at least in Freddy's case, but that seemed like wishful thinking. Maybe a few hours with Joyce from time to time balanced the unsettling home life, but it was difficult to think so.

"Will she work?"

"Maybe."

Joyce opened the oven to remove a tin of cookies. Suddenly she glanced over her shoulder at the clock.

"Kim, turn on the radio. There's something I want you to hear."

"What station?"

"I'll do it." Joyce put the cookie tin on the stove and dashed across the room to flick on the radio. In a moment the room was full of the sound of country-Western music. Joyce lifted a hand to stay Kim's remark. "I don't listen for the music."

"The commercials?"

"You could call them that. Enid told me about it. They call it 'Air Affair.'"

"Good Lord."

"You haven't heard anything like this, believe me."

Five minutes later, Kim could only agree. The announcer, Bud Drabble, in chuckling suggestive tones, was interviewing a caller who identified herself as Joan. Joan was available for dates and the announcer asked what she had in mind.

"Well, I like a steady sort of guy. Someone in his thirties who likes to go places and have fun. Nothing too serious."

"So you're not interested in marriage?"

"That would depend."

"On his being the right guy, right? Does he have to be good-looking?"

"Personality is more important with me."

"What if he's bald?"

"That doesn't matter."

"Okay. A bald-headed man with personality who likes to have fun. What's your idea of fun, Joan? How far do you go on a first date?"

Joan giggled like a schoolgirl although she had said she was thirty-four. "Maybe to first base."

"Aha. Gotcha. Tell me, what idea can we get of you? Put it this way, is there some movie star people are reminded of when they see you?"

"You're kidding."

"What would you say is your most attractive feature?"

"My smile, maybe. And men like my eyes."

"Fair enough. Okay, Joan, we'll see what we can do. You heard her, guys, someone in his thirties, doesn't matter if you're bald, just so you like to have fun. And who knows, you might not strike out with Joan. Sound good? Then call our number and we'll put you in touch with Joan. Now, on with the music...."

Joyce turned off the radio and waggled her brows. "Would you believe it, Kim?"

"Freddy's mother listens to that program?"

"She thinks it's pretty funny. Men call in too. You wouldn't believe what *they* say. Of course, the announcer leads them on."

"Good grief. I'm going up to my room."

"Did you have lunch?"

"I'm not hungry."

Kim gave Freddy a kiss on the cheek and went upstairs with the taste of cookie on her lips. What a program. It was difficult to imagine the depths of loneliness or desperation that would prompt a woman to broadcast to the Chicago area her availability to whom it might concern. How pathetic. Did they give their real names? But surely friends would recognize their voices. It was as bad as the personals column in the *New York*

Review of Books. Kim often wondered if Sister Mary Teresa read those. It was surely possible, given the way the old nun went through their copy. Freddy and Enid. The pathetic Joan on the radio. Suddenly life seemed so sad. Singles bars, broken homes, chuckling idiots like the announcer Bud Drabble — the world was indeed a Vale of Tears when fun was defined as a date with a stranger who happened to listen to an idiotic program. Did Enid Flaherty dream of such anonymous fun?

Seated at her desk, Kim drove away these depressing thoughts and concentrated on the seminar paper she was preparing. Emtee would read it over before she gave it, of course, her criticisms inevitably helpful. Kim still considered herself Emtee Dempsey's student. The nun had hooked her on history when she was a freshman and on the religious life as well, not by what she said but by what she was. Kim had not realized at the time that the Order of Martha and Mary was undergoing a radical change. Her ideal of the religious life remained Sister Mary Teresa, not that she wanted to go back to the habit. She herself had never worn anything more distinctive than a veil, but a veil with ordinary clothes was silly, so she had dropped that too. Being a nun wasn't a matter of clothes.

"The habit is an outward sign," Sister Mary Teresa Dempsey would reply to that. "If clothes are so unimportant, why not wear the habit?"

"No one wears a habit anymore."

An eyebrow appeared above the right lens of the old nun's glasses. No one? As long as Sister Mary Teresa lived, the habit decreed by Blessed Abigail Keineswegs would be worn by one of her spiritual daughters. At least Emtee didn't talk about all the money that could be saved by wearing religious garb. The truth was that they were quite well off, the endowment set aside for the house on Walton Street more than ample to keep the three of them in comfort. In any case, Emtee Dempsey's brief for the habit was not an economic one. Kim wondered what the neighbors thought when they saw Emtee Dempsey emerge in the traditional dress of the M. & M.s each morning when the three of them drove off to Mass. Those who knew her loved her, to the degree one can love a curmudgeon.

Kim remained in her room until nearly six and was surprised to find Freddy still in the kitchen with Joyce when she came downstairs. Joyce was sipping from a handle-less cup and Kim picked up the odor of sherry. Joyce mistakenly thought that her surreptitious cocktails, like her cigarettes, were a secret from Emtee Dempsey. The sound of the television boomed from the front of the house. Emtee Dempsey was listening to the news.

"Want a sip?" Joyce asked.

Kim shook her head. Freddy was seated at the kitchen table filling a piece of paper with crayoned squiggles, Emtee's watch clutched in his free hand. Kim wondered if Enid Flaherty would be able to pry that watch loose from her son.

"I'm going to watch the news."

Emtee Dempsey was enthroned before the set, pulling her upper lip, listening and watching intently. A special report on the local news was devoted to the three bodies of young women that had been discovered over the course of the past weeks. Grisly pictures appeared upon the screen as the announcer spoke. The body of the young woman found in a ravine west of Chicago three days before had been identified as a local divorcée employed in a tool and die plant. She had been raped and strangled and had lain undiscovered for perhaps a week. The announcer re-ran the pictures on the screen. He recounted police speculation that the three murders were connected. Kim was glad when there was a break for the commercial.

"Is that boy still here?" Emtee Dempsey asked.

"With Joyce."

"Wouldn't he prefer to watch television?"

"I don't think the news would interest him."

"I suppose not."

It certainly interested Emtee Dempsey. She sat through

the local and national news and turned away only when the weather came on.

Freddy's mother still had not arrived when Joyce called them to table. A place was set for him as if Joyce had not really expected Enid to come for her son. Freddy was untempted by Joyce's casserole, doubtless because he was full of cookies. Sister Mary Teresa made no concessions to their diminutive guest in the matter of table conversation. Kim made the mistake of mentioning the discovery of the young woman's body and Joyce had fatuously wondered what the world is coming to.

"If you mean, Sister, that you believe there has been an increase in violence proportionate to the rise in population, you are demonstrably wrong. History is a tale of violence. The history of this country is a subset of that tale. Perhaps you mean the difference lies in the fact that we are served up the gruesome details along with pictorial evidence with our supper. There you may have a case that things have changed, but of course the level of shock drops with the rise of what are called the media. However, that murder and assorted mayhem are rampant is scarcely a feature of the times. Sister Kimberly will support me there."

This prediction was not destined to be tested. The doorbell rang and Joyce got up to answer it. Freddy, at the sound of his mother's voice in the hallway, slipped from his chair and ran out of the room. A moment later the three of them appeared.

Enid Flaherty, hands in the pockets of her unbuttoned raincoat, leaned against the door frame and smiled vaguely at Sisters Mary Teresa and Kim.

"You're eating," she said.

"Please join us," Sister Mary Teresa said, perhaps mindful of Blessed Abigail's insistence that a stranger at the door must be treated as one would treat Christ himself. "Joyce, set another place."

"No thanks, Sister. I couldn't eat a thing. Have you been feeding Freddy? I'm sorry. I didn't keep an eye on the time."

"Speaking of which," Joyce said, plucking Emtee's watch from Freddy's pocket. The boy let out a howl and Enid cuffed him gently.

"Let him keep it," Emtee Dempsey said.

"You don't mean that!"

Emtee looked sternly at Kim. "I have a clock in my study and another in my room. Certainly I mean it."

"But it is a gift."

"All the more reason that it should be given."

Joyce looked at Emtee and then at Kim. She gave the watch back to Freddy. In possession of the watch again, Freddy scooted down the hall as if fearful of another confiscation. Joyce went with him. Kim was furious at Enid for not stopping this absurd transfer. The watch was of no earthly good to Freddy. Enid pushed away from the door frame, taking her hands from her pockets.

"I better go. Good-by and thanks."

When she was gone, Kim said, "You shouldn't have done that. He can't even tell time."

"It will give him an incentive to learn. Children love watches."

Kim could not help smiling. Emtee Dempsey's contact with children had been minimal throughout her long religious life but no doubt she had read about them and thus become an expert. The old nun pulled back from the table. She would return to her office for several more hours of work before turning in. Her disciplined life made Kim ashamed of what seemed the unfocused waste of her own. She went down the hall to the kitchen.

"Of course I will," Joyce was saying to Enid Flaherty. "I'd love to. You just go ahead with your plans."

"Can you come to my place?"

"Of course. No problem."

Enid looked fleetingly guilty when Kim came in. "I know it isn't fair but I asked Sister to watch Freddy tonight."

The smell of alcohol was heavy on Enid's breath and her moist eyes were too bright for sobriety.

"No," Kim said firmly. "I'll be your baby-sitter tonight." The NBA playoffs were on that night and Kim knew that Joyce was following the fortunes of the Chicago Bulls.

"Don't be silly," Joyce said and, guessing the reason for Kim's offer, added, "I can watch the game at Enid's."

Enid Flaherty looked glum. "My television is on the blink, Sister."

That did it. Kim insisted and Joyce backed down, but not before having packed some cookies for Freddy to take with him. The boy was tired now and looked ready to go off with anyone. Kim went into the study to tell Sister Mary Teresa where she was going.

"Is it in the neighborhood?"

"Not two blocks away."

Emtee Dempsey frowned and looked at Kim over her spectacles. "Be careful."

Enid Flaherty's apartment was a mess. After they had entered, Enid began to pick up newspapers and magazines that were scattered about, on the coffee table, on the floor, but soon gave up. There was no way she could simply wish away the un-emptied ash trays, the glasses, the bowl in the bottom of which a few sad kernels of popcorn lay. Old maids. She decided that the first item on the agenda was to put Freddy to bed.

Left alone, Kim looked about her in dismay. The drapes in the room were closed as if the schedule of Enid's day bore little relation to the rising and setting of the sun. It was all Kim could do not to set about tidying up the room immediately. That would have to wait until Enid left. In a corner of the room the great gray eye of the television did not blink. Kim had the thought that it had observed more sordid dramas in this room than it had brought to it. The image of the spick-and-span home that Peg, her brother Richard's wife, kept, despite her three young ones, came to Kim. But then Peg had loved ones to inspire her industry and Enid had only forlorn little Freddy.

When Enid emerged half an hour later she was transformed. She wore a simple blue dress, her hair had been brushed and sprayed, and make-up had restored to her face at least the illusion of youth and health. She seemed steadier too and her breath was no longer fragrant with alcohol. Kim wondered if she had imagined that earlier, but knew she had not.

"Well," Enid said, her tone the pleased one of a woman who knows she looks her best. "I'll be going."

"Isn't someone coming for you?"

"We'll meet there."

"There?"

"I can't give you a number to call. We haven't decided where we'll go."

Kim had an intimation of what parents must feel although Enid was at most a year or two younger than herself. She wanted to ask Enid where she was going and with whom and when she would be back. It was irresponsible to leave her little boy with someone all afternoon and then breeze out on the town that night.

Enid might have been reading her mind. She took cigarettes from her purse and sat on the edge of the couch.

"I'm early. It's really nice of you to sit with Freddy. I get so few chances to go out. It's not a lot of fun being cooped up here all day every day."

"You don't work?" Kim asked, knowing the answer.

"Would I be living in a dump like this if I did?" Enid lit a cigarette and exhaled smoke disdainfully. "I'm lucky to be able to keep this place on the money Harry gives me."

"It could be a lot nicer," Kim said carefully.

"Oh, sure. Fix it up, make it nice. Why? It's a hell of a life." Suddenly Enid began to cry. Kim moved closer to her and put a hand tentatively on her arm.

"I'm sorry. I didn't mean to criticize you. Joyce told me you plan to divorce your husband."

"We should never have married." Enid blinked her eyes as if trying to free herself from her burdens. "I love Freddy but I feel guilty for bringing him into the world. Nothing turned out the way we hoped. Harry was awful."

"Your husband?"

Enid nodded. "You were smart not to get married."

Kim bit her tongue. She had not decided not to marry; she had decided to become a nun. Perhaps Enid would not understand the difference. Besides, it was difficult to think of Enid Flaherty's marriage as typical when she poured out her story. The trouble started because there had not been enough money, something Enid attributed enigmatically to Harry's stubbornness, and lack of money meant lack of fun. Had Enid and Harry thought marriage meant an endless date when they would be traipsing from one diversion to another? They had quarreled. Kim could imagine that it was as difficult for a husband and wife to treat each other as real and separate persons as it was for members of a religious order. She could hardly have gone on living with Emtee Dempsey and Joyce for the fun of it. Not that she had any large complaints, but Sister Mary Teresa had her quirks and Joyce was, well, Joyce.

"Then Harry began to drink. I like to drink myself, for fun, but he went overboard. On Friday he would cash his check and by the time he found his way home it was Saturday and he couldn't remember where so much money had gone. There were other women too, though he always denied that was anything serious. Things just happened. Well, they do just happen, in bars. That's why people go to bars. And then he became jealous of *me*. I suppose he thought if he was fooling around I must be too. Have you ever been hit by a man? Of course you haven't. And I mean hit. He just teed off and let me have it."

Enid's eyes were wide with the memory. Kim shivered. Poor Enid. No wonder she lived in such squalor. But what was her future? What was Freddy's? Kim felt unwillingly involved in the troubles of this childlike woman. During the discussions before they sold the college other Sisters had spoken romantically of working with the poor and unfortunate. This is what it came to, Enid and Freddy, and it was heartbreaking. And there were cases infinitely worse. Kim had become a nun with the idea of becoming like Emtee Dempsey, a teacher and scholar. She had never aspired to be a social worker. Now they had no college in which to teach and when she got her degree she would have to apply on the open market. If that didn't work out, she might end up trying to give what help she could to people like Enid Flaherty. Kim felt a little like crying herself.

Enid stubbed out her cigarette and stood. "You see, my life's a soap." She picked up the coat she had tossed on a chair when they came in and slipped it on. "I won't be late."

"It doesn't matter. Have a good time."

Enid's smile was wistful. "I'll try."

It was a relief to get going on the living room after Enid left. Kim checked the kitchen and found it an equal mess. She looked in at Freddy and was glad to see that his room at least was neat. On a toy box against the wall an array of miniature cars was set out. She tucked him in and saw he was holding the watch Emtee Dempsey had given him. The thought crossed her mind that she could retrieve it now in the hope that Freddy would have forgotten all about it in the morning. But she left the watch in his hand.

After she had straightened out the living room, deciding against the use of the vacuum lest it waken Freddy, she turned to the kitchen. Enid's system seemed to be to put off washing dishes while there were still unused ones in the cupboard. Sinking her hands into the hot sudsy water, Kim felt the satisfaction Joyce must feel in keeping the house on Walton Street in order. She was putting dishes in the cupboard when the phone rang. Kim raced to the living room to answer it.

"Who's that?" a man asked after she said hello.

"This is the Flaherty residence."

"The what?" He seemed to be laughing. In the background she could hear voices and music.

"Who is calling, please?"

"Is Enid there?"

"Who is this?"

"This is Harry Flaherty, goddamn it. Is my wife Enid there?"

"No." Kim felt stung by his savage tone.

"Where is she?"

"Out."

"Where?"

"She didn't say where she was going." Kim would not have told him if she knew. This was the man who had actually beaten his wife.

"Who are you?"

"I am Sister Kimberly." Kim straightened her shoulders as she said it and her tone was frostily nunnish. If she assumed the persona of Emtee Dempsey she would be able to deal with Harry Flaherty.

"Sister? You mean you're a nun?"

"That's right."

His tone altered. "Is something wrong?"

"Nothing is wrong. Your wife had to go out and I agreed to watch Freddy."

"Is he asleep?" The reminder of his son softened his voice.

Kim glanced at her watch. It was nine-forty-five. "Of course."

There was silence on the line for a moment. "What did you mean, she had to go out?"

"Mr. Flaherty, Enid went out and I am watching your son. That is all I know."

"Huh. Who did she go out with?"

"She went out alone. Look, I've told you everything I

know. I don't see much point in continuing this conversation."

"You're right. Tell her Harry called."

Kim finished with the kitchen and, when she returned to the living room, opened the book she had brought along, Barbara Tuchman's *A Distant Mirror*. It was almost a pleasure to get out of the twentieth century and read about the Black Death.

When she next looked at her watch it was twelve-thirty. Kim thought of the empty streets outside and of Walton Street, which never seemed to be deserted, day or night, its denizens an oddly mixed group. The street had deteriorated, as what has not, and at intersections were raucous unsavory places whose gaudy lights winked into the wee hours of the morning while sounds like the souls in purgatory emanated from within. Kim did not relish the thought of the drive home at this hour.

It seemed selfish to begrudge Enid her night of vacuous fun so Kim went back to her book. She had begun it on Sunday, two days before, and was unlikely to run out of reading matter before Enid returned. The trouble was that she was sleepy. It was long past her regular bedtime. They rose early on Walton Street in order to attend the seven o'clock Mass at the cathedral and of course Emtee Dempsey had to be hard at work in her study by nine o'clock. Routine, the daily chores, order. How wonderful it seemed by comparison with Enid Flaherty's life. Not many women would envy the life of a nun, even the unusual life they lived on Walton Street, but it seemed to Kim at the moment the best life in the world.

She turned off every light but one and lay down on the couch. She meant to go on reading in that position, but her eyes were heavy. Perhaps if she closed them for a moment...

She was startled awake by the ringing of the phone. It took her a moment to realize where she was. When she did, she lunged for the phone.

"Isn't she home yet?" It was Joyce.

"What time is it?"

"Three. Sister Mary Teresa was worried you'd been

kidnaped and we've been wondering what we'd do for ransom."

"Three o'clock!"

"We think you should spend the night there. What's left of it, that is. Come home in the morning."

That seemed sensible. Kim said so and put down the phone. Sleeping on the couch was not restful and sleeping in her clothes made it worse, but she had no choice.

She sat rather than lay on the couch now, the three-way light beside her at its dimmest wattage. The room, since she had cleaned it up, seemed freed of reminders of Enid. Would she take it as criticism that her house had been made so uncharacteristically neat? Kim turned off the light and moments later the room began to emerge from darkness. Through an opening in the drapes a grayness outside was visible. It was hard to imagine Enid having the fun she dreamed of at such an hour.

Sleep returned when once more Kim stretched out on the couch. She woke to find Freddy standing beside her, looking at her sleepily. How long had he been there? Enid. Kim sat up.

"Is your mama home?"

He shook his head, apparently unconcerned. Kim got up, took Freddy's hand, and went down the hall to Enid's room. It was as she had left it the night before. Good Lord. It was nearly seven in the morning. In the kitchen, a cereal box was on the table and the bowl from which Freddy had apparently had his solitary breakfast. Kim put her hand on his tousled head. Did he always fix his own breakfast?

"Are you full, Freddy? Would you like something else to eat?"

"What?"

"Well, let's take a look."

There were waffles in the freezer that needed only toasting to be ready. Kim put two in the toaster, got syrup from the refrigerator, and sat Freddy at the table after clearing away cereal box and his bowl. There seemed to be no butter. When the waffles popped up, she poured syrup generously over them

and put the plate before Freddy. He ate as if it were his first breakfast. When the doorbell rang Kim was glad Freddy was occupied
with the waffles. God only knew the condition his mother would
be in. Kim remembered the smell of liquor on Enid's breath in
the house on Walton Street the afternoon before.

Enid's key would be of little use to her because Kim
had put the chain on the door. Before unlocking, Kim put her
ear to a panel of the door.

"Enid?"

To her surprise, the doorbell rang again.

"Who is it?"

"Police."

Kim unlocked the door and opened it as far as the chain
would allow. There were two men in the hallway, unmistakably
police, Kim thought, though Richard would doubtless want to
know what she meant by that.

"Yes?"

"Is this the home of Enid Flaherty?"

"Is something wrong?"

"Who are you?"

"Sister Kimberly."

The man who had spoken wore a three-piece suit and
there was a gap between his upper front teeth. He looked at his
companion and then at Kim.

"Sister?"

"Yes. Our house is on Walton Street. I'm baby-sitting
for Mrs. Flaherty."

His lips closed briefly over the gap-teeth. "Could we
come in, Sister?"

His name was Nealy and his companion, squinting
through heavy glasses, was Horst. Their manner was heavy with
a significance it was impossible to ignore. Nealy did not keep her
long in suspense. He suggested they sit, though Horst remained
standing by the door.

"Was Mrs. Flaherty a friend of yours?"

"Was?"

"She's dead, Sister. She was killed several hours ago. She was run over by a car."

Freddy chose that moment to come in from the kitchen. Kim ran to him and picked him up and hugged him tight as if to protect him from the horrible news Nealy and Horst had brought.

Two

Kim would never know what her reaction to the news of Enid Flaherty's death might have been under different circumstances. As it was, she had to absorb the news in Enid's living room with Freddy in her arms. It was impossible to know what the boy made of this intrusion. Kim herself looked at Nealy and Horst as if they were personally responsible for the fact that Freddy was now half an orphan.

"This is her son," she said warningly.

Horst nodded and made a note in the book he had opened. A pained look flickered across Nealy's face and he took Freddy's hand briefly in his enormous one.

"You're here alone with him?"

"Yes."

"Were you here all night?"

Kim nodded. "Look, our house is only a few blocks away. I could phone there and have Joyce come over for Freddy. She's the one who usually sits with him."

"Joyce is a nun too?"

Nealy seemed to be having trouble regarding Kim as a nun. She suddenly felt disheveled and unkempt standing there in the clothes she had slept in. Nor had she brushed her hair.

"What do you mean, your house?" Horst asked.

Kim found herself giving far too lengthy a description of the house on Walton Street occupied by the three remaining members of the Order of Martha and Mary. Why should the police care that it had been designed by Frank Lloyd Wright? She interrupted her chatter to put through a call to Joyce. But it was Emtee Dempsey who answered.

"So you're still there."

"Sister, something dreadful has happened." Nealy had taken Freddy and put him on the floor. Now he led him away. Kim continued in a whisper. "Enid Flaherty is dead. Her body has been found and the police are here."

"May she rest in peace." Emtee Dempsey's tone sounded more like a command than a plea. "How did it happen?"

"I haven't gotten the details yet. Can Joyce come here to look after Freddy?"

"Why don't you bring him here? You have the car, do you not?"

"The police want to talk with me."

"Bring them with you."

Kim sensed that Sister Mary Teresa wanted to be in on any interrogation and she realized that she wanted the old nun's support. There was really nothing helpful she could tell the police but she knew it would take time before they came to see that. She told Emtee Dempsey she'd try and went back to Freddy's bedroom where Nealy was listening to an explanation of the collection of miniature cars.

"Why don't we take him to Walton Street and talk there? Then Sister Joyce can look after Freddy."

Nealy thought about it. Finally he said to his companion, "Sergeant, take the kid somewhere."

Freddy and Sergeant Horst eyed each other and it was clear that neither one of them relished the suggestion. Nealy saw this. He turned to Kim.

"Just a few quick questions. When did you last see her?"

"She went out about eight-thirty." Kim thought of Enid, all dolled up, anxious for a night of fun. "Freddy had been with us at Walton Street throughout the afternoon as well."

"Tell me about it."

It was difficult not making it sound like an accusation. "She left Freddy with Joyce and called for him at dinnertime. Then I came over here and she went out again."

"Where was she during the afternoon?"

"I don't know."

"Do you know if she was with someone?"

"No."

"What about last night?"

"She left alone."

Horst looked up from his notebook. "Did she say where she was going?"

Kim shook her head. She felt as though she were flunking an exam. It was absurd that she knew so little. But there were further questions and further admissions of ignorance before Nealy and Horst made a quick tour of the apartment. They spent some time in Enid's room. Nealy was expressionless when he returned but Horst could not conceal the fact that they were no better informed than before. Freddy had lost interest in the policemen and was playing in his room.

"What happened to her?" Kim asked Nealy. "How did she die?"

"That's what we're trying to find out."

"Was it an accident?"

Nealy looked at her steadily. "We're from homicide."

"Dear God. What did happen?"

"She was struck by a car."

Kim let out a little cry. "But that sounds like an accident."

"Not to the people who saw it happen. Do you still want to take the kid to Walton Street or should we continue here?"

"Oh, let's go there."

But only Nealy followed her Volkswagen when Kim drove off with Freddy beside her. Horst was assigned to check out the apartment and make inquiries of Enid's neighbors. Freddy sat on the edge of the seat, both hands on the safety grip, delighted to be returning to Joyce's kitchen. His happiness seemed mocked by the misfortune that had befallen him. Freddy's unawareness of the true circumstances of this unlooked-for excursion made Kim feel a little bit like God.

Joyce opened the door, exchanged a stricken look with Kim, and took Freddy's hand. Her voice broke when she told him how much fun they were going to have. Emtee Dempsey came out of the study and stood leaning on her cane.

"Are you alone?"

Kim shook her head. Nealy came bounding up the steps from the street and entered the house.

"This way, young man," Sister Mary Teresa said and thumped back into her study.

Nealy was in his forties, it was unlikely that he had taken orders from anyone but a legitimate superior for years, but he started immediately down the hall at Emtee Dempsey's summons. Nealy would have no doubt that now he was dealing with a real nun. It might have been a visit to the principal.

"You'll want coffee, of course," she informed Nealy, already behind her desk. "Sister Kimberly."

"How do you take it?"

"Black."

"Will you have some, Sister?"

Emtee Dempsey scowled. One of her minor crosses was that she was now restricted in her intake of coffee; formerly she had consumed it by the gallon. It had been her mainstay through years of scholarly work. "Ice water." She could have been asking for hemlock.

Freddy was seated at the kitchen table while Joyce skated around the room in worn slippers. There was already a piece of pie in front of Freddy and Joyce was filling an eight-ounce glass with milk. Kim got down a cup and saucer and poured Nealy his coffee from the pot that always simmered in Joyce's kitchen. Joyce came up next to her and whispered, "What happened to her?"

"She was run over by a car."

It seemed best to leave it at that. Joyce affected a tough exterior — she needed it to survive with Emtee Dempsey — but Kim knew what a fragile façade it was. Joyce gripped Kim's arm and her eyes were bright with tears.

"Emtee Dempsey wants ice water."

"Why doesn't she tap her veins?"

But the remark sounded more like a sob than the kidding sarcasm Joyce must have intended. She slid to the refrigerator with a glass and filled it half full of ice cubes. Freddy reached out for it, attracted by the sound of ice on glass. Without hesitation, Joyce gave it to him and took another glass from the cupboard. Kim poured a second cup of coffee for herself and put it on the tray.

During the session that followed in the study it would have been difficult to say who was the questioner and who the questionee. Whatever they might know that the police did not, Emtee Dempsey was intent on learning everything Nealy knew. It was not much.

Enid Flaherty had been struck and killed by a car outside the Tara Beer Hall at approximately two-thirty in the morning. A couple who had been in the Tara and who were seated in their parked car were witnesses. Enid had come into the street and stood there for a moment when a car passed the witnesses. They had been willing enough to talk until it occurred to the woman that their names might appear in the papers as well as in the police report. She was understandably reluctant to have her husband learn she had been out with another man. That seemed to be the kind of bar it was, a sort of singles bar for straying spouses. Emtee Dempsey asked for and received an explanation of the phrase "singles bar."

"A house of assignation," she humphed.

"Well, people meet one another there," Nealy said. He looked at Kim, then looked away. Did he wonder if he should be sullying the ears of nuns with such sordid facts?

"Like the Drumbeat," Emtee said, referring to a bar several blocks away on Walton.

"Exactly." Nealy seemed relieved. "How did you know about that place?"

"Now that we have put convent walls behind us and decided to live in the sea of the people, we have come to know many things, Lieutenant Nealy."

The irony in her voice was light and Nealy did not catch it. But what would he have done if he noticed? The remark was directed at Kim. The M. & M.s had moved to Walton Street with the notion that they would minister to the lay people among whom they would live. Long before the community was whittled down to three this hope had been dashed. The laity proved to be remarkably disinterested in nuns who looked like other women and, in any case, what did the M. & M.s know that could be of help to their neighbors? The bulk of the nuns had swiftly joined the supposed object of their new apostolate and, in the end, it was Joyce who had come to know and befriend their neighbors. Kim said as much now, as addendum to Emtee Dempsey's remark.

"Joyce knew Enid far better than you or I, Sister."

Nealy said, "I want to talk with her."

"And you shall," Emtee Dempsey promised. "But first, what did your witnesses witness?"

The errant wife thought the passing car had blinked its lights at Enid, whether in warning or as a signal. Enid turned and looked toward the car, seemingly waiting. The car accelerated and ran Enid down before she recognized the danger she was in.

"The fact that the car kept going suggests the blinking lights were not a warning."

"A signal then?" Emtee Dempsey said.

"If they blinked. The witness became less sure when she was pressed about it."

The man with her was not at all cooperative. He would not hazard a guess as to the make of the car, he had not noticed its lights blink. If he could have, he would have denied being there when Enid was struck down.

"Did the witnesses know Mrs. Flaherty?" Sister Mary Teresa asked.

Nealy put a thumb on his lower lip as if to draw attention to his separated teeth. "They had seen her in the bar."

"That night?"

"Yes."

"And before?"

Nealy seemed to file the question away. Whether or not those witnesses had met Enid on previous visits to the Tara Beer Hall, it was clear Enid was known there. Jennie Probst, a waitress, as well as one of the bartenders, said she had been there before. Jennie Probst suggested that Enid was a fairly frequent customer.

"And did she meet up with a man on those occasions?" Emtee Dempsey asked.

"The waitress did not remember her being alone for long."

"And last night?"

"She was with a man."

"What did he have to say?"

"We haven't talked with him yet."

Emtee Dempsey stirred in her chair and took a sip of water. The clatter of ice cubes competed with the racket of her rosary beads. Nealy added that they had not yet identified the man Enid had been with. There had been two men for a time and Jennie feared a fight would break out.

"Mr. Flaherty?"

Nealy smiled. "That is our assumption."

"Does he deny it?"

"We haven't located him either."

Kim said, trying to keep her tone even, "He telephoned last night. For Enid." She inhaled and told Nealy the burden of the conversation.

"Did any of you know Flaherty?"

Kim doubted that even Joyce had met him; she herself had not and of course neither had Sister Mary Teresa.

"Were they divorced?"

Perhaps if Kim had known Harry Flaherty personally she could not have given Nealy Enid's portrait of her marriage. The remembered voice on the telephone was disembodied and abstract; she had no face or person to connect it with. But she had a vivid image of Enid as she left her apartment for the last time in her forlorn quest for fun. If Enid was a frequent patron of the Tara Beer Hall and if Harry knew it, the rest of the story seemed clear enough. He could have driven there, waited for her to emerge, and then run her down before speeding away. No wonder the police had been unable to locate him. Kim was sure Nealy had made the same inference. He did not dismiss it when Kim said it aloud. Emtee Dempsey made no comment but her frown suggested doubt. Was the old nun disappointed that the death of Enid Flaherty presented no puzzle to be solved?

The thought seemed uncharitable. Emtee Dempsey was not a woman in need of diversion and eager to seek it in the macabre. Her work kept her busier than most people decades younger than she and Kim was certain Sister Mary Teresa was at least as horrified as anyone else by the violent death of the young woman with whom she had conversed the previous evening.

When the doorbell rang, Kim went to answer it, not wanting Joyce to stop fussing over Freddy. Horst was surrounded by three young women on the doorstep.

"Is Lieutenant Nealy still here?" There was desperation in his voice.

"Where is Freddy?" a thin-faced blonde asked.

"These are neighbors of the deceased," Horst explained.

The neighbors of the deceased had the morning look of those who had had demanding nights. A short stout woman whose mind's eye must have given her a different notion of the jeans she wore than any mirror could, dragged on a cigar-colored cigarette. "We know Sister Joyce," she said, holding the cigarette to her mouth with two stubby fingers. The third visitor was lean and tall, her face dwarfed by the enormous glasses she wore. Kim opened the door and asked them to come in.

In the ensuing minutes a small chaos reigned. Nealy came down the hall from the study as Joyce emerged from the kitchen. At the sight of Freddy, the women rushed into the kitchen gushing and wailing and generally alarming the boy. They put Kim in mind of the witches in the opening scene of *Macbeth*. Horst explained to Nealy that he had thought it best to bring the women along but Nealy seemed to guess who had brought whom. The sound of Sister Mary Teresa's cane thumping down the hall gained the attention of everyone.

To the women in the kitchen she announced that Freddy was perfectly all right with Joyce for now. She pointed Horst down the hall to the study and herself herded the three women there. Nealy and Kim followed as if they were accomplices in this. Emtee Dempsey put them to work bringing chairs from the sun porch so that her unexpected guests could be seated. Orders for coffee were taken and ash trays distributed. At her desk, Sister Mary Teresa took the roll as if this were the beginning of a class.

The blonde was Marge Pollock, the argument against

jeans for chubby women was Audrey Larson, the beanpole with the wide-screen lenses was Terry Stansky. They were all roughly Enid's age, within a year or so of thirty, one way or the other, and they sat like schoolgirls in a row before Emtee Dempsey's desk. Nealy reclaimed the chair he had been sitting in before the interruption and Horst conceded the remaining chair to Kim. He withdrew to a corner and opened his notebook as if it were his shield against the world. Emtee Dempsey studied the three women with a benign smile while Joyce gave them coffee, Freddy at her side. Terry Stansky put her hand on his head and looked around with a tragic expression. If Freddy had managed to get this far into the day without suspecting something terrible had happened, these women must surely have now alerted him. He clung to Joyce's apron and, when she went back to the kitchen, hurried after her.

"I gather that you were all friends of Enid Flaherty," Sister Mary Teresa said and immediately put up her hand. "Not all at once. Please. Lieutenant Nealy and his companion are investigating Enid's death and are intensely interested in anything you might know that will cast light on what happened."

"Harry killed her," Audrey Larson said emphatically and rolled in the embrace of her jeans. The other two nodded like Valkyries over their coffee cups.

"Let us start with you, Mrs. Larson."

"Ms. Larson," Audrey corrected.

Emtee Dempsey nodded agreeably. Kim knew what the old nun thought of that innovation. It was a sign of her curiosity about these women that she did not give them her little lecture on what she considered a trendy barbarism.

"I stand corrected. May I ask if the title conceals a single or married condition?"

They called themselves the MOMSIES, an acronym for My One Mistake Sure Is Enough, a reference to their failed marriages and, apparently, to their determination to keep future relations with men fleeting and temporary. Emtee Dempsey's remark that this suggested a tribute of sorts to monogamy made little impression, perhaps because Audrey was not eager to reveal that the second purpose of their club involved such places as the Drumbeat and the Tara Beer Hall. It was difficult to think of these women as feminists, but it was far more difficult to see them in the role of female libertine. Again Kim thought of the sad expectation with which Enid Flaherty had left her home the night before.

"Was Enid a member?"

"More or less." Audrey sipped her coffee. "She wasn't fully eligible. Her divorce hadn't come through yet. I know you don't approve of divorce, but then, you've never been married." There was a murmur of approval from Marge and Terry. Terry's glasses had slid down her nose, giving her expression a curiously bi-level look. Audrey turned to Lieutenant Nealy. "Have you arrested Harry Flaherty? He threatened to do this and now he's done it."

Emtee Dempsey said, "If he did it you can be sure the police will arrest him and he will pay the penalty. You have heard Mr. Flaherty threaten his wife's life?"

"Enid told us."

"Did she think he was serious?"

Audrey hesitated. "She was still very naive where men are concerned."

"No doubt. Was she in the habit of going to the Tara Beer Hall?"

"I meant naive about Harry. Maybe she thought they would get together again and live happily ever after." Audrey's tone indicated what she thought of that fairy-tale possibility.

"And the three of you were supporting her intention to divorce him?"

"The decision was hers, Sister. We stick together, that's the point of the club, but we're not missionaries. The point is Harry was worse than any of our husbands had been. He wanted to run around himself and then be jealous if Enid so much as glanced out the door of the house."

"Were the Flahertys still living together?"

"Not any more. She made him move out."

"You were their neighbors? Are you all in the same building?"

Only Terry Stansky lived in the same building as Enid Flaherty, on the third floor. Audrey lived across the street and Marge had an apartment in the same building. Marge had a daughter living with her, Terry was childless, and Audrey's son was in the custody of his father, by Audrey's choice. This was a matter of principle with her. Why should her husband lead an untrammeled existence while she was saddled with the child? Emtee Dempsey listened to this theory as if it were one of which she might approve. Nealy looked bored and glanced from time to time at Horst, who continued to write in his notebook. Perhaps he kept a diary while working. Neither policeman acted as if this conference would cast light on the death of Enid Flaherty and Kim was more than inclined to agree.

Audrey said, "We'll take turns looking after Freddy."

"Don't you work?"

Audrey did. She was a clerk in a local outlet of a city-wide dry-cleaning service. Normally she would be at work now, but the killing of Enid Flaherty had set the MOMSIES in motion. A future member of their sorority had been killed and they were determined to do what they could to see that justice was done.

"Were any of you with Enid yesterday afternoon?"

"I was working," Audrey said. "Where was she?"

"Do we know, Lieutenant Nealy?"

Nealy shook his head. Terry Stansky leaned forward and put her empty cup on the desk.

"Enid and I were together. We had lunch in Old Town and then did some shopping."

"Where did you have lunch?"

"We stopped at McDonald's."

"Do they serve drinks?"

"No."

"When Enid came here last evening she had quite visibly been drinking. Was that after she left you?"

Terry pushed her glasses back into place. "We had a couple of drinks."

"Where was that?"

The two women had gone to a succession of bars on the near north side and it seemed obvious that the stop at McDonald's, like the shopping, were euphemisms for an afternoon of drinking. Horst dutifully noted down the bars Terry mentioned. The MOMSIES' idea of liberation seemed to center on the freedom to spend the day and night carousing and cruising.

"What was her mood?" Emtee Dempsey asked. "What did the two of you talk about?"

Terry looked uncomfortable. "Oh, everything. I don't really remember. We just talked."

"About her husband?"

"Some."

"I understand she has spoken with a lawyer about divorce proceedings. Did that subject come up?"

Terry turned to Audrey. "I told Enid about you and Harry, Audrey. I thought she ought to know."

"Know what? What did you tell her?"

"I made it clear that it was him, not you. Enid had to know what he was like."

"What is this all about, Ms. Larson?" Emtee Dempsey asked. Nealy looked less disinterested.

Audrey glared at Terry, but Marge said, "She's right, Audrey. You said how naive Enid was. Why shouldn't she know that Harry was trying to make out with her friends?"

"Fat chance," Audrey snorted. She shook a cigarette loose from a red package and lit it. She still wore an expression of contempt when she looked at Emtee Dempsey but Kim detected an undertone of triumph in Audrey's tone. "He came to the store and tried to make a date."

"Ah. Did he know you were a friend of his wife's?"

"At first? I'm not sure."

"You didn't tell him?"

"I led him on. Of course I knew who he was. He brought in some laundry and then didn't leave and we talked and he asked me if I was married and, you know, went on from one thing to another."

"Did you ask him if he was married?"

"I knew he was."

"Did he know you knew?"

"That was the point of playing him along. I wanted to see if he would mention it. Of course he didn't."

"But he asked you to go out?"

"Yes."

"You refused?"

Audrey drew on her cigarette. "I should have. I didn't want to go out with the creep. But I thought if I went along with it I would have things to tell Enid that would help her make up her mind about him."

"But you were upset that Ms. Stansky told her."

"I wanted to tell her myself."

"Why didn't you?"

"The opportunity hadn't presented itself."

"When did this happen?"

Audrey exhaled a cloud of smoke. "A week ago."

"Where did you and Harry go on your date?"

He had taken her to dinner at a steak house. They had several drinks before dinner and wine with their meal and, over coffee, Harry mentioned that he was married.

"I could see it coming," Audrey said contemptuously. "And it came. She didn't understand him, the marriage was a mistake, he didn't know what to do about it and it was so nice having someone he could talk to about it at last. I led him on. His version had nothing to do with the facts. You would have thought I was the first woman he had propositioned. I felt a little guilty, listening to all that, meaning to tell Enid everything he said."

"You never told him you knew his wife?"

"No!"

"You had seen him in the neighborhood when he lived with Enid, I suppose."

"If I did, I took no notice of him." Audrey spoke as a princess unwilling to acknowledge importuning admirers.

Emtee Dempsey said, "And yesterday was the first time Enid Flaherty heard of her husband's attentions to you?"

"If Terry told her, yes."

"Tell me, Ms. Stansky, did Harry Flaherty ever ask you out?"

"Not likely. He knew Enid and I were friends. Besides, I had known him when they were living together."

"And you, Ms. Pollock?"

Marge looked at the others. "I never told either of you this. He called me a couple days ago. I'm sure it was him. He gave some other name and said he was an insurance agent and Mrs. Enid Flaherty had applied for a policy and he would appreciate it if I would give him some confidential information. At first I thought it was genuine. It wasn't until after I hung up that I realized how strange his questions were. He wanted to know about Enid's personal life."

"What did you tell him?" Audrey looked with disgust at Marge.

"The truth. That Enid was a responsible person, that she lived alone with her son, that she was highly regarded in the neighborhood."

"And that she went out on dates?"

"I said that several men seemed interested in her." Marge looked foolish. "I thought that would help."

"Did you mention the call to Enid?"

"No. I asked her what insurance she had and she didn't know. Harry took care of that sort of thing. It was obvious she wasn't thinking of taking out a policy and I knew I had been tricked."

Terry said, "You should have told her then. Imagine. He takes out Audrey and then checks up on Enid. Just as she always said. Jealous. And violent."

Kim remembered Enid's own portrait of her marriage. Looking at the MOMSIES seated before Emtee Dempsey's desk, she wondered if there were any normal marriages left. The thought was absurd. The MOMSIES, and Enid Flaherty, were scarcely a fair sample. She hoped.

Lieutenant Nealy, thumb on lower lip, said to Terry Stansky, "Were you with Mrs. Flaherty last night too?"

Terry turned to him, the motion causing her glasses to slip again. Her startled eyes seemed to have trouble focusing.

"Who told you that?"

"Ms. Stansky," Emtee Dempsey said smoothly, "you must realize the police already know much and eventually will know all there is to know about this matter. How long were you at the Tara Beer Hall with Enid Flaherty?"

Terry looked around helplessly, seeking something, perhaps she herself did not know what, from Marge and Audrey. Then she burst into tears. Her sobbing confession that she had been inside the Tara Beer Hall when Enid Flaherty was run down in the street outside brought Lieutenant Nealy back into the interrogation. Clearly this was news to him. How had Terry managed to avoid being questioned along with the other occupants of the bar?

"I ran. I went outside with everyone else and when I saw Enid lying in the street, I ran. I went home. I didn't want to stay there. It was so awful. Her body looked so broken and she lay there like a pile of laundry and all those people milling around, curious. It was ghoulish. Of course I thought of Freddy right away but I knew Enid had a sitter. Even so, I stood outside her door for minutes, wondering if I should knock. But what would have been the point of that?"

Nealy said, "Let's talk about the bar before Enid left. Who was she with?"

"Some guy. I don't know. We had been sitting at the bar and he started to talk with us and then he concentrated on Enid so I left them alone. I was talking to someone else anyway. Enid and the guy she was with changed to a table but I stayed at the bar."

"Did you notice when her husband came in and argued with the other man?" Emtee Dempsey asked.

"It wasn't Harry. Was it?"

Nealy said, "A man came to her table and argued with her while she was seated with someone else. Was it Harry Flaherty?"

Terry shrugged her shoulders and her glasses wobbled. "It could have been. I think it was."

"Would you know the man if you saw him again?"

"The man Enid was with?"

Nealy exhaled. "The man who started an argument."

"I suppose. It's dark in there, you know. And we had been drinking all day and it was pretty late."

"When the man with whom Enid went to the table was seated at the bar you must have seen him clearly."

"Him I would recognize, yes."

"But you don't think it was Harry Flaherty who started an argument at Enid's table?"

"No."

"Did you notice him leave?"

"I guess. The bartender went over to shut him up and made him leave."

"What is the name of the man Enid was seated with, the man who had first been at the bar?"

Terry smiled sadly. "Jack something. It wouldn't be his real name. It never is."

"Was Jack still there when Enid left?"

"I don't know. I didn't realize she had gone. The first thing I knew there was screaming and everybody rushed outside and so did I. That's when I saw Enid. I just kept going home."

"You ran?"

"Yes." There was wonderment in Terry's voice. "It must be over a mile and I have no recollection of doing it, but I started to run. I couldn't have run all the way. And then I was in front of my building."

"Who was the man you talked with at the bar?"

"There were several." Again the sad smile.

"You're sure it was Jack Enid was seated with at the table?"

"Sure it was..." Terry's voice trailed away into doubt, calling into question the reliability of her denial that the second man had been Harry Flaherty. Audrey Larson made Nealy's point explicit.

"Terry, you can't see your hand in front of your face in the Tara. Why do you say it wasn't Harry they had to throw out?"

"But it wasn't." The worm of doubt had entered her mind, however, and her words echoed a vanishing conviction.

"Would the bartender know Harry Flaherty?" Horst asked. It was his first question and he had to clear his throat halfway through it.

Terry didn't know and neither did the other two MOM-SIES. Nealy seemed relieved by that. They were interrupted by the ringing of the phone. Sister Mary Teresa answered it and then handed the instrument to Nealy. He took it and did more listening than talking. The three women lost interest in him and began to whisper among themselves. Emtee Dempsey sat back in her chair and looked at the MOMSIES but Kim doubted she was seeing them. What images were created in the old nun's mind by this conversation? She had shown great restraint in not revealing what she must think of the lives the MOMSIES lived. She was perfectly capable of giving them a stern lecture on a saner notion of the dignity of women than any of them seemed to possess, but she had sat through the recital as if she were used to spending the morning with women whose resentment of their failed marriages drove them into bars like the Tara Beer Hall, who could spend an afternoon drinking, and who turned over children to the custody of their divorced husbands, as a punitive move. Nealy put down the phone and did not resume his chair. He spoke to Sister Mary Teresa.

"The car has been found," he said.

"Whose is it?"

"It was stolen and then abandoned. There is no doubt that it is the one that struck Enid Flaherty."

Emtee Dempsey said, "Will you be able to determine who drove it?"

"Let's hope so. But the steering wheel had been wiped clean of prints."

Terry Stansky said, "Harry Flaherty was once arrested for stealing a car. When he was young. He was on probation for years."

"Flaherty has been taken into custody," Nealy said, still addressing Sister Mary Teresa. "At O'Hare airport."

"Is that where he works?"

Nealy shook his head. "He tried to buy a ticket with an expired credit card. The clerk was suspicious and they were holding him out there without knowing we wanted him." Nealy turned to the MOMSIES. "Thank you very much, ladies. We'll be getting in touch with you again." To Sister Mary Teresa he said, "This is an unusual way to question people but it seems to have served its purpose. Thank you for your hospitality."

Horst and Nealy left the study and Terry Stansky got

up from her chair. Still seated, Audrey Larson stubbed out her cigarette. It was at least the fifth she had had since sitting down. "Does Illinois have the death penalty?" she asked.

"That is a penalty we must all pay one day," Emtee Dempsey said.

It sounded like the opening of a homily, an effort to get the MOMSIES to reflect on their silly lives, but she did not go on. The old nun pushed back her chair and stood. Since she was not much over five feet tall, this did not appreciably increase her height. Kim led the trio down the hallway to the front door. Marge went on into the kitchen. In a moment she reappeared. "He isn't there!"

Neither was Joyce. But the inside kitchen door was open. Joyce and Freddy were in the yard, working in Joyce's garden. The MOMSIES stood in the doorway looking out at Freddy.

"The poor little bastard," Audrey said. She glanced at Kim. "Sorry."

Marge said, "Are you going to keep him here?"

Kim nodded. If the alternative was to send Freddy off with one of these three, the boy could stay in the house on Walton Street as long as he liked.

Kim let the women out the front door. Before closing it, she watched them go up the street. Would they have seemed different to her if she had not heard their story in the study? Probably not. But then, Enid Flaherty had seemed just another unfortunate young woman yesterday.

In the study Emtee Dempsey was back at work on her manuscript. It was nearing noon and she was behind on her daily quota of pages.

"Well?" Kim said.

Sister Mary Teresa looked up. "Those three are not ornaments of our sex."

"Anyway, it's over. They have him now."

"The husband?"

"Now that he's in custody, I feel sorry for him. What good will it do if he pays the penalty for killing Enid?"

Emtee Dempsey began to write. She paused and then addressed herself as much as Kim. "None at all if he didn't kill her."

"Do you doubt it?"

A moment went by and then there was only the scratching of Emtee Dempsey's fountain pen. Kim turned and went down the hall to the chapel where she prayed for the repose of Enid's soul. She prayed for Harry Flaherty and for Freddy too. What on earth would become of the boy?

Three

Kim's brother Richard — Captain of Detectives and filled with the pride of office if not its insolence — came by that afternoon, having heard Kim's name mentioned in connection with the death of Enid Flaherty. This displeased him. He was even less pleased to learn that Nealy had permitted Sister Mary Teresa Dempsey to take over the questioning of Enid's neighbors.

"The MOMSIES?"

Richard looked puzzled. "Well, we have Popsy now."

"Has he confessed?"

"Kim, I don't want any of you butting into this. Particularly Emtee Dempsey. We have a nice big police force and we like to do our own work. The fact that you were baby-sitting for the Flaherty woman when she was killed is just one of those things. Nealy was a damned fool to come here in the first place and Horst was a bigger one for bringing those women here to be quizzed by Emtee."

Richard was over six feet tall and had the Moriarity red hair. Red hair is thought to be a sign of wrath and, if that was only sometimes true, Richard was angry now.

"He didn't have much choice," Kim said in defense of Horst.

"He had a choice. And so do you. I don't want to hear that you're interfering, understand?"

"Sister Mary Teresa's interference has been useful to you in the past."

The muscles in Richard's jaw bulged. He could not bring himself to admit that Emtee Dempsey had on several occasions seen what the police had not and so solved their case for them. It did not seem wise to press the point now.

"Richard, Enid Flaherty's son Freddy is staying with us. I have to get into the apartment to get clothes for him as well as some toys. Horst took the key. Can you get it for me?"

"Why the hell is the kid staying here?"

"I was baby-sitting him when his mother was killed. I haven't been released from that. Besides, he and Joyce get along famously. He likes it here."

"In a convent! Why doesn't one of those women look after him? Better yet, we'll contact the relatives."

"Until you do, he'll have to stay here." She told Richard what MOMSIES stood for.

They were talking in the front hallway and now the distinctive thump of Emtee Dempsey's cane was heard. The old nun's face brightened at the sight of Richard.

"I thought it was you. What a delightful surprise. Why are you standing here? Come sit down. Sister, get your brother some refreshments. What would you like, Richard? Beer?"

Richard had an Irish inability to say No to the offer of a drink. "Thank you, S'ter. That sounds good." He actually gave

Emtee his arm and went down the hall with her. Apparently Richard could only be indignant with Sister Mary Teresa in her absence.

The kitchen was empty. Joyce had taken Freddy on a shopping expedition. Kim took a bottle of beer from the refrigerator and carried it and a glass to the study where Richard was bringing Emtee Dempsey up to date on Harry Flaherty.

"Why was he trying to leave town?"

Richard sipped his beer. "Because he was sure he would be suspected of killing his wife. He takes his arrest to be proof that he was right about that."

"Does he deny doing it?"

"Of course."

"What indications do you have that he is lying?"

"For one thing, he can give no satisfactory account of where he was last night."

"What does he say he was doing?"

"Sleeping."

"Well?"

"His bed had not been slept in."

"Perhaps he made it when he rose this morning."

Richard smiled. "You have his story down pat."

"Is it so implausible?"

"It is when the landlady saw him go out around nine and is sure he did not return at any time during the night."

"She must be a very light sleeper."

"She is a landlady. You know he was seen at the Tara Beer Hall?"

"By Terry Stansky? She admits she might be mistaken. Did anyone else see him there last night?"

Richard crossed his legs and looked across the desk. "Sister, I know your curiosity about things like this. But if there was ever an open and shut case, this is it. Flaherty has been arraigned. The District Attorney is certain he can get a conviction."

"The other night on television I saw that yet another young woman had been found dead. How many does that make now?"

Richard stirred in his chair. "Murder is not a rare occurrence. Unfortunately. Sister, let me say to you what I told Kim. I know you're interested in this because you knew the woman who was killed. That does not make you responsible."

"Indeed it does not."

"I'm glad you see that. Leave this to the police, Sister. We've done our job, justice will be served."

"I'm delighted to hear that. I never doubted it for a moment. The fact that so many criminals go undiscovered and their crimes unpunished does not disturb my certainty. God is justice. He is also mercy. You and I are merely human."

Richard was not quite sure how to interpret this philosophical remark. He went back to his beer.

Kim said, "I've asked Richard to let me into Enid Flaherty's apartment so I can pick up some things for Freddy."

"You didn't keep the key?" Emtee Dempsey sounded disappointed.

"I hope you mean that," Richard said. "Okay, I'll get the key and we'll go over there. I'll be with you all the time," he added warningly.

"You must let Sister Kimberly speak to Harry Flaherty as well."

Richard put down his glass with a bang. "Sister, I've tried to make myself clear. I don't want any amateur interference in this."

"I don't blame you. The point is we must let Mr. Flaherty know that his son is with us."

"I'll tell him."

"But he must give us his permission. I want an assurance. He must tell Sister Kimberly that Freddy can stay here with us."

"The relatives can take care of him."

"Tell me about the relatives."

Enid had come from Baraboo, Wisconsin, and Richard understood that her parents were still there. They had of course been informed of the death of their daughter.

"And are there any Flahertys?"

"The town is full of Flahertys. We're trying to find out if he is related to any of them. Harry clammed up after he was arraigned. He'll have a court-appointed attorney since he refuses to make any effort to engage counsel. The lawyer is also trying to locate his family."

"In the meantime Freddy will be with us. If Mr. Flaherty gives his permission."

"Maybe I should take him along with me now."

"Maybe. But as a father I think you will decide not to. The boy is content here. Sister Joyce is a familiar face. It would be cruel to put him with strangers even temporarily."

"Where is he?"

Kim said, "Out shopping with Joyce."

Richard glanced at his watch. He had finished his beer. "If we're going to pick up clothes for the kid, let's get going."

Harry Flaherty had a weak handsome face and there was the look of a cornered animal in his eyes when he looked through the mesh separating him from Kim.

"We spoke on the phone Monday night," Kim said, keeping her voice neutral. "I was watching Freddy when Enid was..."

Across from her Harry shifted in his chair like someone in a dentist's waiting room.

"I didn't do it, Sister. The police don't believe me and they never will but that doesn't change anything. I did not kill my wife."

"They don't believe you slept in your room that night."

"They don't believe anything I say."

"Your landlady says you went out and never returned."

Harry seemed unsurprised. He was a man convinced the world was against him.

"Where were you all night?" Kim asked.

He looked beyond Kim to where a policeman stood guard; there was another behind him, on his side of the mesh. It was possible for Kim to imagine that she was the prisoner and Harry Flaherty the visitor. He leaned toward her, whispering, his voice not quite under control.

"Okay. I was driving around looking for Enid, hitting the bars. After I talked with you and you said she was out I meant to find her. I'm no perfect husband, I know that, but I kept a job, I supported her and Freddy to the best of my ability. You've seen the apartment. Is that such a bad place? Enid wanted a house, but who doesn't? We can't afford a house. What bank would lend me that kind of money on what I earn? Enid was raised in a house with an acre of lawn around it and that is how she wanted to live. In Chicago! I'm a cook." Harry shook his head as if this minor role in life did not fit him.

"And you found her in the Tara Beer Hall?"

He sat back, his expression apparently meant to convey shock. Once more he leaned toward her. "I didn't find her, Sister. I was nowhere near the Tara last night."

"Did you tell the police where you were?" It was like helping a child to lie.

"They want proof."

"Surely, wherever you were, you must have been seen."

Harry shook his head sadly. "You think anyone wants to get mixed up in this sort of thing? Forget about people who saw me."

"Where did you telephone from when we talked?" That was a question Sister Mary Teresa wanted asked.

Harry thought about that, too long, before he said it had been an outdoor booth somewhere along Diversey. Kim remembered the sound of voices and music in the background when he spoke to her. It seemed pointless to tell him that. He was visibly lying.

"An outdoor booth?"

He lifted his head as if to nod, but did not. "No, Sister. That's not true. It was a bar."

"What bar?"

"The Torch."

"And from there you went on to others. What others?"

He listed a string of bars. Kim said, "The police have been told that you came to the Tara and found Enid with another man and started to quarrel but were put out of the place."

"That's not true."

"What bar were you in between two and three o'clock?"

He shook his head. "Do you know where I probably was then? In my car asleep. I was mad and I kept drinking and I must have passed out. The sun woke me up. I was driving to get something to eat when I heard it on the radio. That's the God's truth, Sister."

I was in prison, and ye came unto me. Although Kim did not believe Harry Flaherty, she could not hate him. He and Enid were two sides of the same flawed coin. Enid was dead and now Harry's prospect was prison. Who could take pleasure from the thought of a human being cooped up year after year, ordered about, surrounded by other unfortunates? She could see the child Harry Flaherty had been, the misfit, the outsider, one who had always been caught and punished.

"Freddy is staying with us," she said to him. "Is that all right with you?"

He shrugged. "Why not?"

"Do you have relatives in Chicago?"

"You keep Freddy. That will be best."

"We're delighted to have him for now."

"They're going to get me for this and I didn't do it. That's funny. If I had run into Enid last night I was mad enough

* 55 *

to kill her. Maybe I would have. But I didn't." His lower lip trembled and there were tears in his eyes. "I guess wanting to is as bad as doing it, huh? Maybe I'm being punished for that. I went to Saint Callista's for grade school. What kind of nun are you?"

Kim told him.

"We had Franciscans. Tough as nails." He smiled with an odd nostalgia and again Kim saw the boy he had been. "I knew that catechism like the back of my hand."

"We'll pray for you, Harry."

"Yeah. You better pray for Enid too. She wasn't Catholic," he added, as if that might make a difference.

"Well, did he confess?" Richard asked as they were going out to the car.

"The poor man. He's so pathetic. The two of them were so pathetic. Their lives seem so wasted."

"He's got a lot more wasting to do at Joliet."

"That seems so pointless."

"Maybe we should give him a medal instead."

Kim knew that Sister Mary Teresa would call it sentimental to dwell on the awfulness of Harry Flaherty being pinned up like an animal for the rest of his life. Punishment is not a pleasant thing, it is not meant to be, but Emtee Dempsey could go on and on, condemning those who out of misguided sympathy denied the freedom and responsibility of the criminal. "If I ever murder someone I expect to be executed for it," she insisted. "And I would deserve it. Forget about deterrence and rehabilitation. Those are secondary matters. My offense would be such that no man could forgive me. My crime would be against the race but only God could forgive me. And his forgiveness does not preclude punishment." She was unmoved by reminders of environmental conditions and she considered a plea of insanity the last refuge of the scoundrel. Kim thought Emtee Dempsey had been too long in the orderly setting of her study. If Harry Flaherty had killed his wife it was very likely that he was drunk at the time.

Of course he was responsible for being drunk. Kim let these thoughts go. The simple truth was that Harry Flaherty was locked up and she felt sorry for him. Luckily that was allowed by Emtee Dempsey. "God loves criminals," she asserted. "They are sinners, but we are all sinners."

"Have you found any relatives, Richard?"

"Of his, yes." He groaned. "Harry has three brothers. They still live in Chicago and we have heard from all of them. Harry is obviously the black sheep of the family. Two of his brothers are doctors and the third owns a very successful business. Laundry and dry cleaning."

"Springfresh?"

He had opened the door of the car. "How did you know that?"

"I didn't. There's one near us."

She slid into the passenger seat and he closed the door. When he was behind the wheel he said, "Did he give you permission to keep Freddy?"

"Yes."

"Good. The brothers are demanding that we turn him over. That will be done eventually, I suppose. Unless her relatives contest it." He started the motor and pulled away from the curb, heading for the Flaherty apartment. "The kid will be better off in either case."

When they were at the Flaherty apartment and Richard was unlocking the door, Kim asked if the place were being guarded.

"What for?"

"I don't know."

Inside, the apartment was gloomy and quiet. Richard remarked on how neat the place was and Kim said nothing. He looked around while she went into Freddy's room and began to stack clothing on his bed. There was no sign of Emtee Dempsey's watch, so Freddy must have remembered to carry it with him. Richard came to the door of the room.

"You left the back door open," he said.

"I did not. I never opened it. It must have been one of your colleagues."

"That I doubt."

Kim followed him into the kitchen. The back door was ajar. Richard inspected it. "No sign of jimmying." He went out into the hallway and Kim heard a frightened squeal. It was Terry Stansky, cowering on the stairway. At the sight of Kim she let out a great sigh and rolled her eyes.

"Thank God," she cried. "I heard someone down here and wondered who it was."

Kim introduced Richard as her brother, there seemed no need to mention he was a captain of detectives, and told Terry she was picking up clothes for Freddy.

Richard said, "You say you heard us down here?"

She nodded. "For the past ten minutes I've been debating what to do. I was going to dial Enid's number and see what happened."

"Did you?"

Terry looked confused. "Of course not."

"We've been here less than five minutes," Richard said.

"Oh."

"And the back door was standing open."

Richard started down the back flight of stairs and Terry came into the kitchen. "Does he mean someone else was in here?"

"What exactly did you hear, Terry?"

"The walls of this place are thin as paper and the floors are no better. If I don't have the radio or TV on I always know when people are in. It was the stereo mainly. It came on with a roar and almost immediately stopped. Then I listened and I could hear you moving about."

Richard came back up the stairs, a frown on his face. "Goddamn parasites. They read the obituaries, the society page, get the addresses of people who are away. The paper must have mentioned her address. Not that it would be necessary. The name would be enough. They can look up the address in the phone book. Let's see what's missing."

"Richard is a detective," Kim told Terry.

"Oh really?" Terry threw him a half flirty look and Kim could imagine her at the bar of the Tara.

"Look around with us," Richard said. "You've been in this apartment a lot, haven't you?"

"Practically every day."

But Terry found no evidence of anything missing. The living room was easy, and the kitchen. When they were in Enid's bedroom, it seemed an invasion of privacy and Kim thought of the woman who had slept for the last time here. In a beer stein on the dresser were plastic stirsticks with the names of various bars on them, souvenirs perhaps. Richard noticed that none of the dresser drawers or those in the bedside table were tightly closed.

Terry said, "Sure. That's the way it sounded. Someone rummaging around." She opened the closet door and nodded. Reaching in, she produced a jangling sound. Coat hangers. "I heard that too."

"Anything missing in there?" Richard was opening dresser drawers whose contents were a mess.

"I can't tell," Terry said. "I don't think so."

The sound of jangling coat hangers continued to come from the closet. Terry was entering into the spirit of the search. "All these lovely clothes," she said wistfully. Did she covet them? Kim was looking through a jewelry box full of inexpensive baubles. She closed it and pushed it away. What on earth were they looking for anyway?

Richard called it off after ten minutes, thanked Terry for her help, and rather pointedly led her to the back door. "I'll lock this after you go," he said.

"Bye, Sister," Terry called and Richard shut the door and locked it. He turned to Kim.

"Ready to go?"

"When you are."

Richard dropped her off at Walton Street and when she went in she heard the sound of an authoritative male voice in the study. Joyce was in the kitchen, without Freddy.

"His uncle came. They're in with Emtee. He insists he is going to take Freddy with him."

"I'd better go in there."

The man in the chair across from Emtee Dempsey was in his forties, graying hair worn semi-long, a pipe in his hand, a patient look on his jowly face. His brows lifted when Kim entered and Freddy scooted out.

"This is Sister Kimberly, Dr. Flaherty. One of our nuns."

He rose and bowed. "What a dreadful thing, Sister. I'm sorry you had to be involved in it. I've come to take my nephew off your hands."

"I have been telling Dr. Flaherty that Freddy is no trouble at all. Did you speak to his father?"

"Yes. He wants Freddy to stay here for the time being."

Dr. Flaherty smiled. "I had no idea nuns were so eager to have children underfoot." He sighed. "I suppose you'll want me to clear this with Harry." He looked at Kim. "How did you manage to talk with him?"

"Haven't you spoken with him?"

Dr. Flaherty looked pensive. "It's easier saying this to nuns than it would be to strangers. Harry has led a troubled life, I really don't know why. He is the youngest of four brothers and in most ways had more opportunities than the rest of us. He seemed to resent that. Perhaps he felt he had to compete with the rest of us. He was a great trial to my mother, God rest her soul. The fact is we haven't seen Harry in years. We learned of his marriage after the fact. We were asked to the baptism of his son. That is the only time I ever saw the child. It was useless to offer him financial aid." Dr. Flaherty looked directly at Kim. "Do you think he did this dreadful thing?"

"He denies it."

"I believe him. I can't imagine that he would kill anyone, let alone his own wife."

Sister Mary Teresa said, "He will need a good lawyer."

"And he will have one. My brothers and I will spare no expense. There is no way we can keep this out of the papers, that damage is already done. Proving him innocent will clear the slate."

Was it unfair to think that Dr. Flaherty's main concern was the adverse publicity?

He said, "Did you two know Harry?"

Emtee Dempsey shook her head. Kim said, "Sister Joyce may have met him. I don't know."

"The fact that nuns have volunteered to look after his son is a plus. Needless to say, I will defray any expenses you incur."

Kim dismissed this but Dr. Flaherty shook his head.

"No. It is the least I can do. Perhaps you will be called upon to testify. I understand you were looking after Frederick when this tragedy occurred."

Kim said she was. Would Dr. Flaherty be happy if he knew what she would have to reply to any questions about what Enid had said before leaving the apartment? Dr. Flaherty stood.

"My wife attended your college," he told Sister Mary Teresa.

"Really. What class was she in?"

"She didn't graduate, actually. But she was there for nearly two years."

Everything he said seemed part of an effort to enlist them in some unspecified campaign. He put his pipe in his mouth and puffed but it had gone out. He was looking pensive again.

"My wife is shocked to hear where Harry's wife apparently spent her evenings after she and Harry broke up. No doubt this kind of violence can be expected around that kind of dive. I simply do not understand young women nowadays."

Emtee Dempsey made a noncommittal sound. Kim showed Dr. Flaherty to the door and was relieved to get him outside without the necessity of presenting him to Joyce. Joyce would not have appreciated his apparent effort to make Enid Flaherty look like a trollop in order to save his brother and the Flaherty reputation. When Kim returned to the study, Emtee Dempsey had not resumed her writing.

"Tell me about your day, Sister Kimberly."

Emtee Dempsey was curious about the setting in which Kim had spoken with Harry Flaherty and nodded through the recital of Harry's accounts of his whereabouts the night his wife was killed.

"He should tell the police everything. It is silly to lie to them. Each time they catch him in a lie the worse trouble he is in. Did you think he was lying to you?"

"About his whereabouts last night?"

"Yes."

"I don't know. He does not inspire confidence, Sister. He is a weak, self-indulgent person. Spoiled. He clearly expected Enid to meet standards he himself scoffed at."

"Where is the car he claims to have slept in?"

"I gather he drove it to the airport."

"Did you tell Richard what he said to you?"

"No."

"You regard it as a confidence?"

"Maybe. Maybe I don't believe him."

"If he is lying again, it would be well to know that. But what if he is telling the truth? You are not bound by secrecy if what he told you could save him from unjust punishment. There is nothing particularly shameful about getting drunk and falling asleep in his car. Surely it would be preferable to have that known than to be accused of murder. I wonder if he isn't counting on you to tell the police."

"I didn't get that impression. He seems almost willing to be punished for something he says he didn't do."

"What is Richard's number?"

Kim dialed it for her and sat while Emtee Dempsey suggested to Richard that Harry Flaherty's automobile should be carefully examined for evidence that he had spent the night in it. Kim could imagine Richard's reaction at being told how to conduct a murder investigation. For some time Emtee Dempsey held the phone to her ear, listening, saying nothing, her eyes closed.

"You do have Harry Flaherty's car though? Good. No, I suggest nothing of the kind. He may be as guilty as you think, and he may not be. You would not want a clever defense lawyer to produce evidence that Harry was somewhere else when Enid was killed. I gather you have found nothing incriminating in the car that ran over Enid."

More listening, though this time she did not close her eyes. When she hung up the phone, she smiled at Kim. "It is not always easy to be a dutiful citizen."

"He'll check it out, Sister. You can be sure of that."

"It won't matter. How can you prove someone slept in a car?"

"I have no idea."

"It would be far more important to find that he had not been where he was said to be. Was it Harry Flaherty who argued with his wife at the bar less than an hour before she was killed?"

"Are you assuming he is innocent?"

"No. The courts must, of course. No, I tend to think Harry Flaherty is guilty. But I do not see how he can be convicted. When Terry Stansky is cross-examined, she will admit she is not sure she saw Harry arguing with Enid in the bar. What else have they? A broken marriage, a jealous husband, threats, and the car that killed her. It would not take much of a lawyer to get a jury to doubt that Harry Flaherty was at the wheel of the car. He has to be shown to be its driver and how can that be done? Do you know what I would do if I were you?"

"What?" Kim said without enthusiasm. Emptee Dempsey had sat forward and there was a gleam in her eye.

"This may be why God permitted you to drop distinctively religious garb. You could not do it otherwise."

"Do what?"

"I would like to know what that waitress, what was her name, Jennie something or other, Probst, the one in the Tara Beer Hall, would tell you about last night and the argument at her table that involved Enid Flaherty and two men."

"You want me to go to a place like that!"

"There will be photos of Harry Flaherty in the afternoon editions. They had nothing this morning, but Katherine Senski assures me they will find one. That will enable Jennie Probst to speak with more assurance.

"Why would she speak to me?"

"Ask if she would recommend that you apply for a job there. That should set the scene. You can mention the death of Enid Flaherty and one thing will lead to another."

From the vantage point of Emtee Dempsey's study the outside world was a remarkably simple place. No wonder Richard got angry with her. The trouble was that her views and judgments of the world she scarcely knew often turned out to be uncanny in their rightness.

"You think I can prove that Harry Flaherty is innocent?"

"Or that he is guilty."

"There is nothing I could learn that the police won't find out."

"Sister Kimberly, you should never underestimate your ability to draw people out. Jennie Probst will speak one way to the police and quite another to a young woman curious about her work."

"I cannot deceive her."

"Don't. I wouldn't hear of it. You will be putting a hypothetical case to her. I am assuming that you do not really aspire to be a waitress. But perhaps you do. There would be many opportunities to minister to the unfortunates in the Tara Beer Hall."

Sister Mary Teresa's tone was only faintly teasing. She was not above saying I told you so when the altered mission of the M. & M.s was mentioned. She had fought the sale of the college and ridiculed the romantic ardor with which the apostolate to the poor and underprivileged had been promoted. Her counter-suggestion that an experimental year be devoted to this work involving only a small group of nuns had been ridiculed in turn. But the old nun could take little pleasure in having been right now that the college was no more.

Upstairs, Joyce was settling Freddy into the guest room. Kim looked in on them.

"What time is it, Freddy?"

He looked at her blankly.

"Where is your watch?"

He thought about it, then shook his head. "I don't have it."

"Did you lose it?"

Joyce said, "I haven't seen him with it today. Maybe he left it at home."

"Maybe."

But Kim was sure the watch had not been in Freddy's bedroom. Emtee Dempsey's gift of it to Freddy seemed as sensible as the errand to the Tara Beer Hall.

"I'm going honky-tonking, Joyce. Too bad you can't come along."

"You sound like that awful program. 'Air Affair.'"

"I mean it. Emtee wants me to go to the Tara Beer Hall and talk to the waitress who served Enid and her boy friend last night."

"You're kidding."

"I wish I were."

"She can watch Freddy and I'll go with you."

"Now you're kidding."

"What will you wear?"

"What I have on."

"A suit? I wonder. You could consult the MOMSIES about proper attire."

"I'll go just the way I am."

"Well, you can't go now. It's after four and you'd miss dinner. Besides, she wouldn't be there, not unless she works twenty-four hours a day. You'll have to go much later."

It seemed almost a reprieve. Refusing to go was a species of stubbornness. She did not want to tell Sister Mary Teresa that the thought of strolling into the bar filled her with repulsion as well as fear. Besides, what if she should meet a MOMSIE there? Emtee Dempsey apparently gave no thought to the scandal that might be occasioned by a nun in a singles bar. And then the evening news made the expedition pointless. Harry Flaherty had confessed to killing his wife and plea bargaining was in the offing.

Emtee Dempsey, on the sun porch before the set, leaned forward and raised a hand for quiet, though neither Kim nor Joyce had spoken. The story was attributed to an unnamed source but what was for attribution was Dr. Michael Flaherty's announcement that Jay Gilby had been hired to defend his brother. Gilby, a legendary figure in the Chicago criminal courts, could have gotten Judas Iscariot off with a reprimand, or so Emtee Dempsey summed him up when the news broke for a commercial.

"Dr. Flaherty certainly wasted no time. Perhaps one of the other brothers was busy on that while he was working on us."

"What did he want?" Joyce asked.

"Character references, I think. Did you ever meet Harry Flaherty, Sister Joyce?"

"No."

"Then you can know little bad about him from your own experience. You will make a good witness."

"I don't want to be a witness."

"A subpoena will give you no choice."

This mild teasing suggested to Kim that Emtee Dempsey was not at all happy with the news story. Over dinner she began to doubt the source of the story.

"But you don't know who it is."

"It's as plain as can be. The Flaherty brothers. It tells us what they intend to do, what Dr. Flaherty indicated they intend to do, namely get the story off the front pages as quickly as they can. They seem willing to sacrifice their brother's freedom if they can pack him away under a lesser charge. The question is, will they be able to persuade Harry to go along. Sister Kimberly?"

Emtee Dempsey considered Kim an expert on the accused because of her brief conversation with him. "I said he was a weak man."

"Where's my mom?" Freddy had been busy with his meal and his question silenced them all.

"She wants you to stay here for a while, Freddy," Joyce said. "Don't you like us?"

"I like my mom."

"Of course you do."

It was a difficult moment and Emtee Dempsey had little to contribute. She brought her coffee to her lips and kept it there. She was allowed two cups a day, one in the morning and another in the evening, but no deprivation could explain the length of time she held it to her lips.

Freddy came with them when they went to chapel to say Compline. He sat like a little man, waiting patiently for them to finish. Did he even know what prayer is? Kim's heart went out to him. His mother dead and his father on the way to prison. Would life with his wealthy uncles make up for that?

Some hours later, after Joyce had put Freddy to bed, Kim looked into the study to tell Sister Mary Teresa she would be working in her room. Her seminar paper would never get written this way. Emtee Dempsey looked surprised.

"I thought you were going to the bar."

"What's the point of it now?"

"I talked with Katherine Senski again. She shares my skepticism about that news report. Nothing has changed."

Katherine Senski, a reporter on the *Tribune*, had been a trustee of their college and had fought at Sister Mary Teresa's side in the attempt to save it from the iconoclasm of the younger nuns. Now the two old women consoled each other that events had proved them correct in their opposition. Emtee Dempsey's appetite for news was never fully assuaged by newspapers and television and Katherine Senski was more than willing to fill her in on news that had not made it into print. Joyce came down and heard Emtee Dempsey suggest that Kim go have her talk with Jennie Probst.

"I'll go with her, Sister. Nuns should always go about in pairs."

"An excellent idea," Emtee Dempsey said. "Is the boy in bed?"

"He is. If he wakes up you'll have to soothe him."

"Of course. I shall stay up until you return."

"Who knows?" Joyce said. "I may get a job. My line is going to be that I want to be a go-go dancer."

Emtee Dempsey looked sternly at Joyce. To them both, she said, "Go — go."

Four

The name of the bar suggested that entertainment would be provided by a harpist or tenor, even by bagpipes, but the music that met them at the door of the Tara Beer Hall was country music, the kind featured on "Air Affair."

"Maybe they're all from the western counties," Joyce said.

They stood in the entrance, peering into the gloom. Weak spots sunk into the ceiling illumined cones of smoke, the bar shone like a solitary planet in an ink-black sky, and at the far end a trio of urban cowboys twanged and banged and wailed into their microphones. Silhouetted along the bar were huddled customers indifferent to the heart-rending ballads amplified to such a decibel level that the very atmosphere seemed to vibrate in 4/4 time. Joyce took Kim's hand and led her into the dark.

"I can't see a thing," Kim protested.

"Good. That works both ways."

An apparition loomed in the darkness, a waitress in a uniform that glowed in the dark. Joyce asked for a table.

"Sit anywhere you like," the flat cheerful voice said.

"We can't see."

"You'll get used to it."

The apparition drifted away. A male voice called "Good evening, ladies" in the intonations of Bela Lugosi. Joyce's grip tightened on Kim's hand and they moved deeper into darkness. They found an empty table by colliding with it. Receiving no answer to their apology, they sat as if sinking into anonymity.

"I wish Emtee Dempsey were here," Kim said with gritted teeth.

"I don't think this chair would support her."

"This has got to be the least brilliant idea she ever had."

"Even the dumbest."

A waitress suddenly glowed before them. "What'll you girls have?"

"Beer," Joyce said, and a list of brands was recited. Joyce named one and the glow faded.

Kim said, "I don't want beer."

"I doubt that they have champagne."

Kim's eyes were growing accustomed to the darkness and she became aware of other people around them. Hardly visible figures took on shape and she could see that at some tables there were only men, at others women. A minority of couples. The deafening music continued, the numbers punctuated by halfhearted applause. Their beer arrived and Kim could make out a woman behind the glow of the uniform.

"Is Jennie Probst here tonight?"

"Who's asking?"

"I'd like to talk to her."

The figure bent toward Kim. "Are you another cop?"

"No. Is Jennie here?"

"What do you want to see her for?"

Joyce said, "You're Jennie, aren't you?"

"If you knew why did you ask?"

"We're friends of Enid Flaherty," Kim said. Emtee Dempsey's suggested ruse seemed all wrong now that they were here.

"We took turns baby-sitting her little boy yesterday."

"You two belong to those MOMSIES?"

"We know them," Kim said. "But we don't belong."

"I'm working. I can't talk now."

"Do you get a break?"

Jennie laughed joylessly. "Sure. If I trip and break my arm. And, believe me, that is possible here. Can you see better now?"

"A little."

"That's about as good as it gets. Look, when there's a lull I'll be back. That's six dollars for the beer."

"Six dollars!"

"I know. You're paying for those cowboys and the chance you might meet someone. You interested? I got a nice table of guys back there."

"No. No, we just want to talk. Come back when you can."

"Couldn't I at least see who I'm refusing," Joyce said when Jennie had gone away.

"Joyce!"

"Joke. Here's to crime." Joyce lifted her glass and drank. Kim wished she had asked Jennie to bring her a coke instead. Joyce was entering too thoroughly into the spirit of the place. No, that wasn't fair. Joyce was a kidder and thank God for that. Their lives would be a lot less fun without her.

Fun. This was the place where Enid Flaherty had come in search of fun. She was as likely to get a sun tan here. It was obvious that any identification made in these surroundings could be questioned and that diminished the importance of talking with the waitress, Jennie. If she ever came back. There was an illumined clock over the bar and Kim was not sure it was working, time passed so slowly. She was almost surprised to find that the hands had moved on to read ten o'clock.

Joyce said, "Are you going to drink your beer?"

"Do you think you should?"

"On my night out? Of course."

When Jennie came back she asked if they were ready for another round. Kim said No before Joyce could speak. Jennie seemed relieved and pulled up a chair. When she lit a cigarette her pale pointed face came brightly into view, eyes concentrated on the flame. She extinguished it with an enormous exhalation of smoke.

"So what do you want to talk about?"

"What happened here last night, Jennie?"

"Good God, don't you read the papers or watch TV?"

"Sure. But not all of it makes sense. For instance, the quarrel."

"You sure you're not cops?"

"Positive."

"Look around you. What can you see? It was this way last night. It's this way every night. You have to be half owl to work here."

"But there was a quarrel, wasn't there? You were quoted in the paper."

"Yeah. With my name misspelled. My one chance for fame and my name's misspelled."

"Who was Enid with?"

"Some guy. She met him at the bar so at least she knew what she was getting. They came back to that table over there."

"Do you know the man she was with?"

"If you're not cops, you're just as bad. I've been answering questions like that all day and they tell me they're not through with me yet. Sure I know him. By sight. Names? In here names don't mean a damned thing. He calls himself Jack." Jennie's cigarette glowed as she puffed on it.

"He's not here tonight, is he?" There was a tremor in Joyce's voice.

"I haven't seen him. Geez, I hope not. That would be pretty awful, wouldn't it? After what happened. Not that I'd be surprised. It wasn't as if he knew Enid."

"Did she come here often?"

"Some. Sometimes early, sometimes late. When my shift starts, the lights are on and there's the last of the sunlight coming in. It's cheerier then, but then of course you can see what a dump it is. Those are the ones you know, the ones you've seen by natural light. Most of my customers I wouldn't know if I passed them in the street during the day."

"Did Jack ever come early?"

"Not that I know of. But he always started at the bar. People at the bar have faces. Back here, they're only voices. And hands." Her cigarette glowed again.

"Was it her husband who came in and argued with Enid?"

"Who knows? That's what the cops seem to think."

"You must have seen his picture in the paper. Was that the man who started the argument?"

"His picture was in the paper?"

"Tonight. Both the *Trib* and the *Sun-Times*."

"No kidding. There must be a copy at the bar. I'll take a look."

"How long have you worked here?" Joyce asked.

"Don't ask. The money's good, believe it or not, and that makes the hours and the customers worth it."

Kim said, "Could you take a look at tonight's paper?"

"I said I would. Let me finish my cigarette, okay? Can you see what I'm wearing? I guess not. Tennis shoes. Ask any waitress, the worst part of the job is what it does to your feet.

The trouble is your feet sweat in tennis shoes." Jennie sighed. "What do you girls do?"

Joyce said, "I'm a cook. She types."

"You're a secretary?" Jennie sounded impressed.

"Sort of."

"She takes dictation," Joyce said. "But who doesn't?"

"Yeah. You're right. Who doesn't?" She pushed away from the table. "I'll be back. Can I bring you another beer? Those guys would buy you one if you want me to ask."

"We'll pay for our own," Kim said.

"Okay. Same thing? I'll be back."

And she was gone before Kim could stop her. "We don't have to drink it, Joyce."

"At three dollars a bottle? What's the difference? You're driving."

It would serve Emtee Dempsey right if Joyce came back tipsy from this excursion. Kim wasn't going to begrudge Joyce a minor indiscretion. The problem was, when Jennie returned with two more bottles of beer, they didn't have six dollars. They had four ones and change.

Jennie said, "Don't worry about it. I'll make it up before the night's out."

"Just leave one," Kim said. "Could you do that?"

"Why not?"

"Did you get a look at the paper?"

"Yes."

"Was Harry Flaherty the man who started the argument here last night?"

"Did you see the picture?"

"What's wrong with it?"

"It looks like a high school graduation picture. All posed, necktie. That isn't the way I see people here."

"Then you don't think it was Harry Flaherty?"

"I didn't say that. It could be. But I wouldn't swear it on a stack of Bibles."

"Terry Stansky thought it was Enid's husband."

"I read that. But she was really smashed last night. So was Enid, for that matter. I think they'd been at it all day. Terry would have seen at least two Harry Flahertys if he was in here last night."

"Couldn't the police see that?"

"It's not her identification that matters. Mr. Hennessy, the manager, was the one who recognized him. He and Lenny threw him out. Mr. Hennessy was positive about it and he would know. Apparently Enid's husband has been in here lots of times."

"It's funny his name wasn't in the paper."

"No it isn't. He's mad enough that she was killed right outside the door. What kind of publicity is that? I guess sightseers have been going by all day but look at tonight. Normally we have a much larger crowd."

"Is Mr. Hennessy here now?"

"It's too early for him. You'll have to stay until after midnight if you want to talk to him."

"It doesn't really matter," Kim said.

"Poor Enid." Jennie sighed. "I liked her. But it's sad, coming to a place like this. Women are married a couple of years and get tied down to a house and kids and they think all kinds of wonderful things are happening. Somewhere. So they break up and come out for a look and what do they find? The Tara Beer Hall. It's sad."

They left their four dollars and change for Jennie. Outside it was bright by comparison with the interior of the bar. They walked in silence to where Kim had parked the Volkswagen. When they got in, Joyce said, "I meant to ask her what material her uniform was made of."

"Why?"

"Wouldn't you like a dress that glowed in the dark?"

When they got back to Walton Street, Katherine Senski and Sister Mary Teresa were on a couch in the living room, a sleepy Freddy between them.

"He said he was frightened," Emtee Dempsey said.

"Poor little fella," Joyce said. "Come on, Freddy. I'll take you upstairs."

"Sister Kimberly." Katherine looked stern. "How is your graduate work progressing?"

"Just fine, until recently. Sister Mary Teresa has taken a personal interest in the death of Enid Flaherty since her child was in our care when his mother was killed. Tonight she sent Joyce and me out bar hopping."

"I don't believe it."

"You shouldn't," Emtee Dempsey said. "Youthful hyperbole. Sister Kimberly was good enough to volunteer to speak with the woman who waited on Enid Flaherty last night. Did you succeed, Sister?"

"The woman is a waitress in a singles bar called the Tara Beer Hall."

"I've read of it," Katherine said. "I thought she worked nights."

"She does."

"You actually went to that bar?"

"Hyperbolically speaking, yes."

"Good grief. The place is a den."

"Have you been there, Katherine?" Emtee Dempsey drawled.

"Not very likely, my dear." A silence fell. Kim was not supposed to know of the long unrequited passion Katherine Senski had nursed for a former managing editor of the *Tribune*, now retired. Emtee Dempsey had told Kim the story as an example of the imitations of the vow of celibacy which abound in the world. The old nun marveled at the asceticism and self-denial put at the service of the acquisition of wealth, artistic success, and athletic excellence, not to mention romantic ends. Everyone knew of such cases, yet everyone professed to find the vows of a nun mystifying though they were undertaken for the greater end of all, the pearl of great price. Katherine Senski had kept her heart pure and her body inviolate in the doomed hope that one day that managing editor would turn to her and, in a shock of recognition, see in her the love of his life. He continued his bachelor existence in a condominium on the north shore, devoting his days to chess and the complete works of Thackeray. Even in what she would have called her salad days Katherine would not have gone within a stone's throw of a place like the Tara Beer Hall.

Katherine said, "The Tara Beer Hall has figured prominently in stories of that young woman's death, Sister Mary Teresa. Like your own, my knowledge of it has been gained by reading."

"Sister Kimberly, describe the place for me."

Kim did, in vivid detail, her eyes serving to feed the mind of Emtee Dempsey. Of course she kept to essentials. There was no need to mention ordering beer or Jennie's offer to fix her and Joyce up with a table of nice guys. Emtee listened with attention and, when Kim was done, shook her head.

"If some poor creature were made to frequent that place as a matter of judicial decision, committees would be formed to protest such cruel and unusual punishment. Why would anyone voluntarily spend more than two minutes in such a place?"

"There are many lonely people," Kim said. "Remember Enid Flaherty."

"I do. Katherine, have you any knowledge of this man Hennessy?"

"Not unless he's related to the maker of cognac."

"Ah. Not a very subtle hint. Sister, would you get our guest a stimulating beverage? Do we have brandy?"

"I think there's some sherry."

"Sherry will be fine," Katherine said. "Just a dollop. Will I be drinking alone?"

"You will unless Sister Kimberly cares to join you."

Kim let that go and went into the kitchen. Joyce kept the sherry in a small cupboard over the refrigerator. There was not much more than a dollop in the bottle. She poured it out for Katherine.

"Good Lord, haven't you had enough for one night?" Joyce had come into the kitchen.

"My hand won't stop shaking."

Joyce did not join them and when Kim settled down, Katherine Senski returned to the reason for her visit. She had begun her account of the three Flaherty brothers but had been interrupted by Freddy. Now she resumed, beginning with Dr. Michael Flaherty.

Michael Flaherty, M.D., in his early fifties, was the eldest brother. He had done his undergraduate work at Notre Dame and attended the University of Illinois Medical School, interning at Cook County Hospital. After a year in general practice in a suburban clinic, he did a residency in pathology at the Mayo Clinic and, upon his return to Chicago, joined an already flourishing group of pathologists. Upward mobility characterized his life. He had a summer place near Lake Geneva, a home in Winnetka, a schooner on the lake, and belonged to half a dozen clubs in the greater Chicago area. His golf handicap was 7 and he was an avid racquetball player at the Chicago Athletic Club. It would have been difficult to imagine a life more distant from that Enid had described as hers and Harry Flaherty's. The confident handsome man who had sat in Emtee Dempsey's study that afternoon fitted the profile perfectly.

"Does Harry strike you as a man of such principle that he would refuse help from his brother?" Emtee Dempsey asked Kim.

"He is refusing the lawyer his brothers engaged for him," Katherine said.

* 78 *

"Why?"

"Does stubbornness qualify as principle?"

"A nice question," Emtee Dempsey conceded. "Not when it is linked to stupidity. Does he long to be convicted?"

"Patrick Flaherty has done less well, but he too is both prosperous and prominent."

A graduate of DePaul, Patrick Flaherty attended Northwestern Medical School, after which he was drafted into the Army. He spent a year in Vietnam and after his discharge returned to his alma mater for a residency in obstetrics. A leader in the Right to Life Movement, high in the councils of the Knights of Columbus and Serra, his practice was divided between the affluent and the needy. He had delivered Enid's baby gratis. He had tried unsuccessfully to persuade Harry to pursue a career as a medical technician, with an eye perhaps to employment in Michael's lab, but Harry had insisted on doing unskilled labor. Dr. Patrick Flaherty's impassioned opposition to capital punishment had recently appeared in the Sunday Magazine of the *Tribune*. He lived in Oak Park, where he was a leader in the effort to preserve that historic suburb. He was the brother who had tried unsuccessfully to persuade Harry to accept the services of Jay Gilby.

Emtee Dempsey had been frowning while Katherine talked. "I think I was unfair to Michael Flaherty earlier today. He has every right to wish to preserve the family's good name."

Kim said, "Whose idea was it for Harry to plead guilty and bargain for a lesser charge?"

"That would have been Dennis Flaherty," Katherine said.

"Tell me about him," Emtee Dempsey asked.

Dennis Flaherty had been an entrepreneur since his student days at Loyola. He had started a food service that delivered pizza and spaghetti to dorms and in his junior year had gone into competition with the university laundry service. This effort eventually became Springfresh, with branches throughout the Chicago area.

"Audrey Larson works in one of them," Kim said.

"Who is Audrey Larson?"

"A friend of Enid's. One of the MOMSIES."

Katherine winced when the strange term was explained to her. Like many women who had succeeded in a man's world, she was ambivalent toward the women's movements, which struck her as attempts to buttress mediocrity. She was somewhat like the tycoon who does not understand why everyone has not become a millionaire. Kim always found it wise to avoid discussing such subjects with Katherine. Nor was she now about to take up the cudgel on behalf of the MOMSIES. Katherine returned to her profile of Dennis Flaherty.

Dennis, far more than the other brothers, had tried to help Harry, offering him any number of jobs in his burgeoning organization. At thirty-six, Dennis was the closest in age to Harry and he could not understand why his young brother refused to board the rising rocket of his far-flung business. Katherine made it clear that Harry could easily have been living a life similar to his brothers'. But he adamantly refused help from them.

"He seems deficient in sibling rivalry," Emtee Dempsey observed.

"There is a darker reason," Katherine said. "One of our reporters got a hint from a jail guard and checked it out. It has to do with the mother."

Mrs. Bridget Flaherty had as a widow raised her four boys, and was understandably proud of the accomplishments of Michael and Patrick and Dennis. Doubtless she had put them before Harry as models and they were the measure according to which his shortcomings were gauged. Harry had done poorly in school, although this had nothing to do with his capabilities. His intelligence tests showed that he had talents equal to his brothers. But an antic streak had shown itself early and, in high school, manifested itself in the theft of a car. This felony had followed by a week the gift of a car by his brothers to Mrs. Flaherty. Harry refused to drive it. His mother's reaction to his misbehavior — he got off with probation — must have made her seem an ally of his older brothers. Harry joined the Marine Corps after graduation from high school and, like Patrick, spent a year in Vietnam. He returned home sullen, aggrieved, and even more alienated from his family.

"Why?" Emtee Dempsey said. "I do not understand him."

"He was adopted," Katherine Senski said.

"Ah."

"Mrs. Flaherty, as used to be customary, chose not to tell him, and the adoption assumed the status of a family secret. When Harry discovered the truth, on the occasion of joining the Marine Corps, his hitherto aimless opposition to his brothers became a settled policy. He even began proceedings to change his name."

"To what?"

"Harry Nemo."

"Hmm. Did he have Latin in school?"

"A smattering. And some Jules Verne, I suppose."

Emtee Dempsey said, "I begin to understand Harry Flaherty. He felt anonymous. And an impostor too. Who were his parents?"

"I don't know. Would it matter?"

"I suppose not."

"None of the brothers approved of Harry's marriage. The girl was not Catholic and the three Flahertys are ferociously loyal to their faith. Harry must have thought being a Catholic was an imposture too."

"Yet he had Freddy baptized," Kim said.

"I would like to speak with Harry Flaherty," Emtee Dempsey said. "The case against him is curiously flimsy." She looked at Kim. "That waitress Jennie could not identify him as the man who raised the fuss with Enid an hour before she was killed?"

"No. And she dismisses Terry Stansky's guess. It doesn't matter, however."

"Indeed?"

"Remember the manager, Hennessy. Jenny says he is sure it was Harry Flaherty."

"He alone has the eyes of a night bird?"

"'The Owl of Minerva flies only at midnight,'" Katherine Senski murmured.

"Hegel?" Emtee Dempsey looked at Katherine.

"Did he say that?"

"You're being facetious. Sister Kimberly, you will have to speak with Mr. Hennessy."

"I am not going back to that bar."

"Why should you? Does he live there? You might even approach him directly, through Richard. Failing that, we will fall back on Katherine. I would like to have a sense of the kind of man Hennessy is. Imagine, being manager of a bar like that. Why should his word be reliable?"

"Because he is not happy to have the place known for the wrong kind of misbehavior."

"I find that unpersuasive."

Katherine said, "I will take the Hennessy assignment."

"Good girl."

"Girl? Elderly hyperbole."

Later, in her room, lying in bed and watching images in her window travel across the ceiling as traffic passed below, Kim considered Emtee Dempsey's interest in the death of Enid Flaherty to be a pointless reflex rather than an inquiry that could lead to an explanation other than the obvious one. Of course Kim had had the advantage of talking with Harry. How many accused persons admit their guilt? Harry sounded sincere when he denied killing Enid, but by his own admission he could not have been sober last night and in the cool light of day it would have been easy for him to deny the deeds of his drunken self.

Seated side by side on a couch in Viewing Room B of the Philpott Mortuary, Mr. and Mrs. Schneider, Enid's parents, looked more bewildered than grieved. The body in the open coffin at the far end of the room was a tribute to the mortician's art but they had difficulty connecting it with their memories of their daughter. Mr. Schneider frowned and leaned forward when Kim spoke, watching her mouth. Mrs. Schneider repeated everything into his ear. "Deaf," she mouthed to Kim. It was three-thirty Thursday afternoon. The Schneiders had been driven down from Baraboo, Wisconsin, by their son Donald, who stood sullenly in a corner of the room wearing his Sunday suit. The MOMSIES had tried to put him at ease but he nodded without speaking and finally they gave up. Joyce was crossing the room toward him, weaving among the scattered groups of people. Kim, feeling the Schneiders were being neglected, had drawn a chair up to their couch.

"Your grandson is staying with us for the time being," Kim said, and waited until Mrs. Schneider, like Echo, had relayed this to her husband.

"Why?" he asked.

"The boy was with them when it happened," Mrs. Schneider said twice.

"Why?"

"I was baby-sitting," Kim said.

Mr. Schneider got it the third time and looked at Kim suspiciously. Several times his eye had gone to the cross she was wearing on a chain around her neck. Kim saw no reason to tell the Schneiders she was a nun.

"They are neighbors of Enid's," Mrs. Schneider said. She looked toward the end of the room and then brought her eyes back. When the old couple stood before the open casket for a few minutes, the only sign of emotion had been Mrs. Schneider's reaching out for her husband's hand. Then they had come to this couch and remained there.

"Where are you staying?" Kim asked Mrs. Schneider.

"The Holiday Inn. Donald has stayed there before."

"Do you come to Chicago often?"

Mrs. Schneider shook her head vigorously. "Donald visits from time to time. I can't imagine why. I hate Chicago."

Mr. Schneider did not catch her last remark and she repeated it loudly. People turned to look at her. She lifted her upper lip to reveal a row of very even, obviously unreal teeth, and then her mouth became a line again. Michael Flaherty came to speak to the Schneiders and Kim left him alone with them. Joyce came to her side.

"Donald is a barrel of laughs," she whispered to Kim.

"Most people are at funerals."

"For him life is a funeral."

"What did he say?"

"Nothing. Is he a mute?"

"His father's deaf," Kim said irrelevantly.

"A matching set. I wonder what Dr. Flaherty's saying to them."

The MOMSIES—Audrey, Terry, and Marge—joined them, encircling the nuns as if to fend off intruders. Audrey's eyes were wet, Terry snuffled, and Marge looked stunned. They had just come from the casket.

"Three days ago she was alive," Marge said.

"I've never been to a funeral before." Terry patted her nose with a handkerchief. "It's awful. Barbaric. What's the point of displaying her like that? I want to be cremated and forgotten."

Marge put her arm around Terry's shoulders. Audrey's lip trembled. The MOMSIES were the only ones showing obvious sorrow at the death of Enid Flaherty. Terry moved away from Marge.

"My God, there's Jack."

A medium-sized man, a thin gold necklace showing at his open collar, stood in the doorway of the viewing room. His thin hair was teased and sprayed and a large mustache drooped at the corners of his mouth. When he saw the MOMSIES, he crossed the room to them.

"Hello, Jack," Terry said, her voice cool.

"My name's Greg."

"Greg what?" Kim asked, but he ignored her. He had seen the casket and was drawn to it. His walk was a rolling bow-legged one and his arms seemed unnaturally long.

"Greg," Terry said disdainfully. "I know he said his name was Jack."

"This isn't the Tara," Audrey said. "I think it was nice of him to come."

Someone touched Kim's arm and she turned to face Dr. Flaherty. He drew her away from the others.

"We are having Masses said for her, of course." He looked expressionlessly around Viewing Room B as if surveying a pagan rite. "I'm here to represent the family. We thought it best to keep things low key. The Schneiders are pleasant people. Who is that looking at Enid now?"

"Greg."

"Greg what?"

"I don't know."

Dr. Flaherty studied her face as if seeking signs of complicity. "One of her boy friends, I suppose."

"Have you met Donald?"

"Does he have a last name?"

"Enid's brother. There, in the corner."

Dr. Flaherty looked at Donald for a moment. "I'll talk to him later."

"I understand that Harry did not admit killing Enid."

His eyes brushed over her. In profile, he said, "Plea bargaining may be his best option."

"He denies killing Enid."

"I know. That won't do him any good."

Hennessy's identification of Harry Flaherty as the man he had thrown out of the Tara Beer Hall Monday night an hour before Enid was killed had been released to the press on Wednesday. Hennessy gave a vivid account. Harry Flaherty, drunk and enraged, had threatened to kill his wife. "I'll get that bitch. I'll kill her," were the words Hennessy remembered Harry shouting when he was hustled down the sidewalk away from the entrance of the bar. It was an occupational hazard, Hennessy said philosophically: estranged spouses meeting at his place and under the influence of a few drinks flaring up at each other. But Harry Flaherty had been different. "I believed the guy. He sounded as if he really meant it. Obviously he did." Why had not Hennessy alerted the police or Enid? More philosophy. What difference would it have made if he had? Drunken threats seldom lead to arrests.

Richard had brought the story to Walton Street before it appeared in the papers. He had heard of the visit Kim and Joyce made to the Tara Beer Hall. He was more sad than angry. They talked in the kitchen. He did not want to argue with Sister Mary Teresa.

"Kim, stop playing games. We've got this wrapped up and it's ridiculous for the two of you to be going to a place like that, going over well-covered ground. I know you want to see Harry pay for what he did. Don't worry. He will."

"I wonder if he did it."

"Well, don't. Hennessy, the manager of the Tara, is positive he was there and threatened to kill his wife. An hour later she was dead. It was no accident she was run over. Who else would want to do such a thing?"

That was the major difficulty with Harry's claim to innocence. Who else had a motive to kill Enid? There was something even worse than Hennessy's identification, however. A handkerchief with Harry Flaherty's laundry mark had been found in the car that killed Enid, wedged between the front seats. With that, Kim's willingness to entertain the possibility that Harry was telling the truth dissipated.

"All right," she said to Richard. "I'll tell Sister Mary Teresa."

The old nun received the news without visible surprise. She nodded. She still held her fountain pen and seemed ready to resume writing.

"I told Richard we wouldn't interfere again."

"Interfere?"

"He thinks you're trying to prove Harry innocent."

"I received a call from Katherine. About Hennessy. An odd coincidence. In college, he was for a time Dennis Flaherty's partner in his campus fast food service."

"All the more reason he would recognize Harry."

"Yes," Emtee Dempsey said thoughtfully.

The old nun did begin to write again and Kim took away with her the implication in Sister Mary Teresa's voice. But it was silly to imagine that his adoptive brothers would frame Harry when they were so obviously panicked by what had happened. The trouble with conspiracy theories is that they accommodate all irksome facts. Like the handkerchief. That could have been put in the car by the one who actually drove it. But if the Flaherty brothers had wanted to rid themselves of the embarrassment of Harry, he would have been the victim, not Enid.

Now, in Viewing Room B, talking with Dr. Michael Flaherty, remembering the sketches Katherine had given of him and Patrick and Dennis, it was impossible for Kim to imagine the successful doctor as part of a plot to engineer anyone's death.

A minister had been engaged by Philpott and the ceremony now began. Reverend Castor had never known the deceased so his remarks were necessarily general ones. He read Psalm 23, said a few things about the inevitability of death, and counseled the several dozen people before him to look to the future. His message seemed to be that, with the passage of time, they would forget what had happened and their lives would resume their normal course. That is what Enid would have wanted.

When he was done, Philpott and an assistant came forward to close the casket. There were a number of sobs when the lid was lowered over the waxen face of Enid Flaherty. Kim breathed another prayer for the unfortunate woman and, with the others, filed out of the building and into the parking lot. The Schneiders would go in one of Philpott's cars. As it turned out, only half a dozen vehicles made the long journey. As the mourners grouped themselves around the open grave, the MOMSIES once more stood with Joyce and Kim. Mr. and Mrs. Schneider and Donald were on the opposite side of the grave. Terry Stansky nudged Kim and nodded. She might have been indicating the Reverend Castor, who had taken up his place at the foot of the casket, which had been rolled onto the device that would lower it into the grave. Then Kim noticed Greg, pulling at the ends of his mustache and looking ill at ease. Another man stood beside him. Kim looked questioningly at Terry.

"I'll tell you later," she whispered.

Perhaps she would have, if Donald Schneider had not broken down. The stolid man stared at the coffin and his expression did not really change when a sob broke from him, apparently against his will. Then tears began to roll down his face and his shoulders heaved. He cried uncontrollably and the sight of the powerful man weeping like a child affected them all. Kim felt a lump in her throat and Joyce cried openly. The MOMSIES huddled together and wept. Mr. and Mrs. Schneider looked at Donald and the others as if they did not quite understand what was happening. Against a background of weeping and lamentation, Reverend Castor read a burial service. He read swiftly, slurring words, obviously anxious to get away from there.

Afterward, he shook hands with the Schneiders. Mr. Schneider got out his wallet but Philpott interposed himself.

"That's all taken care of," he said, casting a glance at Castor.

Castor went hurriedly away across the grass to his car and soon others followed suit, as if they were bent on escaping the grief they had displayed.

Emtee Dempsey listened to Kim's account of the funeral at table that evening. Freddy was not with them. He was the guest of his grandparents and uncle at their motel. Donald, after breaking down at his sister's grave, had found his voice and excited Freddy with talk of the pool at the Holiday Inn. Freddy would stay the night with the Schneiders and be dropped off at Walton Street the next day before they headed back to Wisconsin.

"Greg was the man Terry was with the night Enid was killed?"

"Apparently. He called himself Jack then."

"And there was another man with him at the cemetery?"

"Yes."

"Describe him."

Was this just the old nun's usual curiosity about the wider world she seldom entered or was she persisting in her hope to show that, whatever tack the official police investigation took, it was likely to be wrong. This was a settled theory of hers and it was difficult to dismiss, since she had frequently shown it to be well founded.

"Sister Kimberly, the police mind is a professional mind and is not immune to the familiar dangers of narrow expertise." The way she said the last word indicated her distaste for it. "I could illustrate what I mean in my own field of history, or in medicine, or in science. We become the victims of past success. A method that has worked well before tends to be trusted blindly and we resist anything that calls it into question. Progress in science is made by those who thumb their noses at received opinion and narrow orthodoxies. Consider Albert Einstein."

"And Freud?" Kim teased. Emtee Dempsey considered the father of psychoanalysis one of the architects of modern disorder. When she pronounced his name it came out Fraud.

"Fair enough. The great deviants, too, support my view. The point is that police procedure is just that, a procedure, a method, a trusted modus operandi. By and large, it deserves that trust, but it must be employed with a skeptical eye all the same, for who is to say when the exception will arise?"

"And you think Harry Flaherty is an exception?"

"People are always exceptions. Theories about human behavior must take that into account. This applies with special force in the investigation of a murder."

"Most murders present very little difficulty so far as identifying the murderer is concerned."

"True. But each is interesting in its special way. You will say that only Harry Flaherty had a motive to kill his wife. What was it? Jealousy? He may have been jealous, but he had been jealous for a long time, according to your friends the MOM-SIES. Why did his jealousy spur him to kill Enid early Tuesday morning? Why hadn't he killed her a week before, a month before? Jealousy is too vague. What was the nature of the quarrel in the bar when Harry came to Enid's table?"

"So you do not resist Hennessy's testimony?"

Emtee Dempsey ignored that. "Who was Enid seated with? Describe the man who stood with Greg or Jack in the cemetery."

Such leaps were permissible over the dinner table on Walton Street. Kim thought of the man Terry Stansky had directed her attention to. What was striking about him was his ordinariness. It was a warm day, but he had worn a tweed sport coat and trousers of a solid color. His face in three-quarters profile seemed ascetic: almost hollow cheekbones, thin nose, a jutting chin. What was not ordinary was his hair. It was luxuriant, dark, almost blue-black, concealing the man's ears.

"A wig?" Emtee Dempsey sat forward.

Kim laughed. "I have no idea."

"Maybe he was a cop," Joyce said.

"Were there police at the cemetery? Were there police at Philpott's?"

Neither Kim nor Joyce had recognized any, if they were there.

"You must ask Richard if there were."

"I don't think he'd appreciate the question."

"The answer is almost certainly no. They will no longer be troubling themselves about the Enid Flaherty murder. Doubtless a very junior person in the District Attorney's office will be assigned the case and now not even he will be susceptible to proposals for plea bargaining. The case is open and shut. After we have made our visit to chapel, you must telephone the Stansky woman. If she drew your attention to that man, she must know who he is. I want to know."

Terry Stansky did not answer her phone and Kim was glad. But only for a moment. Terry might have said something that would puncture whatever balloon Emtee Dempsey was attempting to inflate. The old nun's motive seemed merely to oppose what she took to be the police verdict on Enid's death. She had no alternative explanation and her interest did not seem to encompass any real concern for Enid or Harry Flaherty. She did not know Harry and she had met Enid only once. Perhaps that is what permitted her to treat the killing as an intellectual game at which she could beat the police. Joyce and Sister Mary Teresa were in the living room when Kim returned from phoning.

"She isn't home."

"Too bad."

"Kim and I could run over to the Tara Beer Hall and see if she's there."

For a crazy moment, Emtee Dempsey seemed to take Joyce's suggestion seriously. "No. Try her again later. If you can't reach her tonight, try in the morning. Or you could drop by." Her brows lifted at Kim's impatient sigh. "When you take the Schneiders to see their daughter's apartment."

Richard had let her keep the key of Enid's apartment when Kim told him she would have to be returning for other things of Freddy's.

"But you will have reached Terry Stansky by telephone before then."

Kim tried Terry's number again before going to bed but received no answer. The thought that the MOMSIES were out on the town on the very day of Enid's funeral made Kim more impatient than Emtee Dempsey's persistence. Audrey and Terry and Marge would spin out of the orbit of Walton Street now and Kim did not regret it.

In the morning she waited until after nine before trying Terry's number. No answer. Sister Mary Teresa frowned.

"Go over there."

"But she doesn't answer the phone."

Emtee Dempsey pushed back from her desk and with the aid of her cane rose to her feet. "I'll come with you."

Kim could not believe it. It was always a bit of an expedition when Emtee Dempsey left the house. The old nun did not relish the difficulties she had getting around and her morning excursion to Mass was a major trip. The cane was all right in the house, but she did not use it on the street and thus relied on the support of a companion.

"You don't have to, Sister. I'll go. But there is no point..."

Emtee Dempsey thumped out of the study and went down the hall with what for her was full speed. Nor did she leave her cane in the elephant-foot stand near the door. Pulling the door open, she was on the front porch before Kim could tell Joyce they were going out.

"She's going with you?"

"That's what she says."

Joyce crossed her eyes and took a pack of cigarettes from the pocket of her apron. "Have fun."

Emtee Dempsey stood at the end of the walk, waiting impatiently for Kim. Passengers in passing cars stared wide-eyed at the little nun dressed in a way that had been normal in the time of the Blessed Abigail Keineswegs but in present-day Chicago was a traffic stopper. Kim opened the door of the Volkswagen and began the considerable effort of getting Emtee Dempsey inside. The major trouble, once she had been steered backward into the car, was the headdress. The starched winged headdress was as wide as the door, and the low ceiling had not been built to accommodate such millinery extravagances. Despite her small size, Emtee Dempsey had to slump in the seat. She glared out at Kim as if this nuisance had been her idea. Kim closed the door on her carefully but firmly.

Terry Stansky's apartment was on the third floor, there was no elevator, and the stairs were steep, but Emtee Dempsey could not be dissuaded from making the climb. Kim let her go first, prepared to arrest her fall if the old nun tumbled down the stairs. There was much huffing and puffing but it was clear that Emtee Dempsey was now as determined as a pilgrim mounting the Scala Santa in Rome. This seemed an excessive expenditure of energy to obtain the answer to one question from Terry Stansky.

"If the answer is right, I will have other questions."

They were resting on the landing outside Enid Flaherty's door. Kim suggested that Sister Mary Teresa wait there while she brought Terry down, but, grim-faced, Emtee Dempsey shook it away.

"I have come this far. I will go the rest of the way."

There was more resting now, but she climbed relentlessly on. When they reached the third floor, Emtee Dempsey leaned against the wall. Her cheeks were flaming. She closed her eyes and breathed heavily.

"Going down will be easier."

Emtee Dempsey opened one eye in wordless comment. For the moment she wanted to forget those stairs even existed.

"Which door is hers?"

"I'll see."

There were only two doors — one apartment on each side of the building. The door without a name had to be Terry's, since the other read Whittier. Kim knocked and was surprised when the door swung open. Emtee Dempsey brushed Kim aside and waddled into the room, looking around swiftly, her great headdress performing like a trained bird. She went through the living room and down a little hall to the kitchen. She came to a stop in the doorway and her shoulders drew back.

"Dear God in heaven."

Terry Stansky lay upon the kitchen floor, on her side. Her eyes were open and her discolored tongue stuck out. Around her neck was a twisted nylon stocking. Terry Stansky was dead.

Five

Sister Mary Teresa had never had such a vantage point before. Throughout the medical examination of the body and through much of the routine going-over of the apartment, the old nun, in the full panoply of Blessed Abigail Keineswegs' prescribed habit, sat in a straight-back chair, hands folded over the handle of her cane, following the proceedings with intense interest. And she kept quiet. For the most part. She could not be expected to sit silently when Richard lit into Kim.

"Captain Moriarity," she gruffed. "You are speaking nonsense. We discovered the body, we did not murder the woman. You should thank God we had enough sense to come over here when the phone went unanswered. You might not have known of her death for days."

"You should have notified me."

"Bosh. And would you have dispatched squads of men to find why Mrs. Stansky did not answer her phone? You are jumpy because you know what this murder does to your previous assumptions."

Richard glared at her, but did not rise to the bait.

Terry Stansky was pronounced dead and it was estimated that she had been dead for at least twelve hours. Kim wondered if things would be different now if she had come to see Terry yesterday rather than relying on the telephone. She did not need Emtee Dempsey to tell her that was foolish. Either Terry would not have been home or her body would have been discovered some hours sooner.

"When did you last see her alive, Kim?" Richard had gone away after Emtee's remark and now came back, apparently intent on starting from scratch again.

"At Enid's funeral yesterday. She was at Philpott's and came to the cemetery too. All the MOMSIES were there."

"All?"

"Well, all three of them."

When Marge came over from across the street, Kim went downstairs to talk to her. Marge had been in a dazed condition at Enid's funeral but this second death was almost more than she could bear. The rubber bag containing Terry Stansky's remains was carried by as they talked and Kim distracted Marge's attention from it.

"We're being punished," Marge said in a husky whisper.

"What do you mean?"

"God is punishing us. I've never felt right about joining the club. It seemed so . . ." Marge shook her head. She could not find the word and did not really care. "Enid. Now Terry. Does Audrey know?"

"She will. Where did you go from the cemetery yesterday?"

"Me?"

"Didn't you leave with Audrey and Terry?"

She had. The three had taken the long way home, going leisurely along Lake Shore Drive, talking about Enid and what a rotten life she had had. Marge looked at Kim. "Can you imagine what it was like living with those parents of hers, and then she comes to Chicago and marries Harry and look at that. Now it's all over. What kind of life is that? Terry said..."

But now Terry too was dead. Kim put her arm around Marge's shoulder and walked her back across the street.

"Why don't you tell Audrey, Marge."

"She's working at Springfresh."

"Then go to the store. She shouldn't hear about Terry from a stranger."

Marge did not look eager to bear the tragic news to Audrey or to anyone else. "They stayed together last night. I had to get home, but Audrey and Terry decided to eat out. This will be more of a shock to her than it is to me."

Kim did not tell Marge she and Audrey would be questioned endlessly, far more than they had been in the investigation of Enid's death. Emtee Dempsey had said it. The case against Harry Flaherty was seriously weakened by the murder of Terry Stansky. And it had been murder. Emtee Dempsey listened carefully to the first attempts to reconstruct what had happened.

The door had not been forced and there was no sign a struggle had taken place prior to the strangulation of Terry Stansky.

"If she let him in, she must have known him."

"Him?" Emtee Dempsey asked.

"The assailant," Richard corrected, not looking at her.

"Who might have been waiting for her in the apartment when she came home."

"There's no sign the door was jimmied."

"The back door?"

"Either door. That doesn't mean someone could not have entered without a key, of course."

When the telephone rang, silence fell. Everyone's eyes turned to the phone and odd thoughts churned the mind.

"Answer it, Sister Kimberly," Emtee Dempsey said and, there being no objection, Kim picked up the phone.

"Terry, is that you?"

"Joyce? This is Kim. Why on earth did you call here?"

"The Schneiders have arrived. They brought back Freddy. I think they would like to see Enid's apartment."

"That's not such a good idea at the moment."

"Something's wrong?"

"Uh-huh. Could you convince them to just leave Freddy with you and put off visiting the apartment?"

"Donald has been telling them exactly that. I think he wants to hit the road."

Richard and Nealy were visibly impatient during this. Emtee Dempsey, with the aid of her cane, got to her feet. Joyce was asking, "Can you tell me what it is?"

"I think we'll be home very soon. I'll tell you then."

She put down the phone and Emtee Dempsey said, "Sister, there is nothing more we can do here."

Richard was so glad to see them go that he provided two burly officers to help Sister Mary Teresa down the stairs. They all but carried her down and she did not protest. But she shook free of them when they were on the walk outside the building.

"The Schneiders are at the house," Kim told her.

"Good. I want to meet them."

The Schneiders were standing on the porch of the house on Walton Street when Kim and Sister Mary Teresa drove up. Donald was off getting the car gassed up in preparation for the trip to Baraboo and his parents were anxious to be on their way.

The sight of Emtee Dempsey, when Kim had pried her free of the passenger seat, clearly nonplused them. Freddy ran down to the old nun and offered to take her cane.

"I'll need it to get up those stairs, boy."

Kim got an arm under Emtee's elbow and levered her up the stairs. Mr. Schneider, his mouth literally open, stared at the old nun, then looked at Joyce and Kim. That set the tone for the next twenty minutes before Donald drew up to the curb and tooted for his parents.

The Schneiders' abiding concern was that Enid had not "turned." When she had written to tell them she was married, she did not mention that Harry Flaherty was Catholic and it had been a severe blow to them when they found out.

"What is your religion?" Emtee Dempsey asked. She had settled into a redwood chair and persuaded the Schneiders they would be more comfortable seated. Mrs. Schneider took a chair but her husband sat on the swing. His mouth remained half open as he stared at Emtee Dempsey's weird clothing. He seemed not to hear the tinkling of the chains as he rocked back and forth on the swing, seeking equilibrium in the presence of a nun.

The Schneiders belonged to the church of a free-lance evangelist who had gravitated north and whose ability to see the news of the day as foretold in minute detail by the Good Book fascinated the Schneiders and the other members of his small rural congregation. Mrs. Schneider went on a bit about Reverend Skillen, perhaps to make it clear where she and the mister, and Donald too, stood on matters of religion. Their preacher seemed to favor eschatological topics and his longing for cosmic punishment in terms of all-out nuclear war had communicated itself to the Schneiders. The end is near. Kim had the feeling that Catholicism was seen as a target of divine wrath by Reverend Skillen. For the Schneiders to be waiting here, however nervously, with a nun dressed as Sister Mary Teresa was, must be an experience more harrowing than to have to bury their daughter.

When Donald arrived, the Schneiders headed for the car with alacrity. Joyce went down with them and Emtee Dempsey thumped into the house. Minutes later, Joyce came up the stairs with Freddy's hand in hers.

"Well, now they know the worst. What was going on at Terry Stansky's?"

They got Freddy settled in the backyard and, over coffee in the kitchen, Kim gave Joyce the news. She took it about as well as Mr. Schneider had the sight of Emtee Dempsey in her habit. Joyce shook her head slowly back and forth.

"You found the body!"

"There was a nylon twisted around her throat." Kim let it go at that. No need for Joyce to know what the face of a victim of strangulation looks like.

"It can't have been her husband," Joyce said through the fingers of the hand she had pressed to her mouth. "He's in Saudi Arabia."

This fact was stressed on the noon news on television, in the afternoon editions of the Chicago papers, and by Katherine Senski when she called Sister Mary Teresa. In the course of several days, two young residents of the same Chicago building had been killed. Enid's husband had been arrested and arraigned with unusual speed, but the death of Terry Stansky could not be explained by a jealous husband. Her apartment had not been robbed, there was no sign of personal assault. Whoever had killed her had come to do just that and, having done it, left. Why? Who would want to strangle Terry Stansky? A large number of police were assigned to the case, questioning her friends, reconstructing the last hours of her life, seeking any lead that would help. Given the infuriating connection to the house on Walton Street, Richard assigned himself to question the three nuns.

"It may simply be a fluke," he said. "There may be no connection at all between her death and Enid Flaherty's." Richard spoke without conviction.

Emtee Dempsey cleared her throat. It was the only

comment she felt that nonsense deserved. They were in the study at the old nun's insistence. She did not see why this interview should take long and she was anxious to make up lost time on her manuscript. Richard drew something from his pocket and put it on the desk.

"Your watch, Sister. You left it in Terry Stansky's apartment. That's quite an inscription."

Emtee Dempsey gave no sign of surprise. "Thank you. A class of students who confused elation at leaving college with gratitude for the little they had learned from me. I assume you have sent people to the Tara Beer Hall."

"That ground has been pretty well covered, but we'll go over it again. Someone had it in for both women."

Kim said, if only to get her mind off the puzzle of Sister Mary Teresa's watch, "Audrey Larson and Marge Pollock should be given special protection. If someone killed both Enid and Terry, well..."

"Nonsense," Emtee Dempsey said, but Richard nodded.

"Kim's right. They are vulnerable."

"Very well," Emtee Dempsey said. "Have them move in here for the nonce."

"It would be a lot easier to guard one place than two."

"Richard Moriarity, if you want the advice of an old nun, it is this. Presuming a connection between the two deaths, do not look for a common motive as if the order of the deaths could have been reversed. Proceed on the assumption that Terry died because of something that occurred during the investigation of Enid's death. Something that rendered her vulnerable."

"Meaning she might have found out who Enid's killer is?"

"Perhaps without even knowing that she knew."

"That's just a guess."

"What is not at this point? It is a guess that the two deaths are connected. It is a guess that some malevolent person is bent on killing the surviving friends of the deceased. If you don't mind, I have more important things to do at the moment than indulge in guessing games."

They adjourned to the kitchen, Joyce and Kim and Richard. Richard accepted the offer of a refill.

"Will you release Harry Flaherty now?" Joyce asked.

"No. There is still a strong case against him."

"Have you spoken with him, Richard?"

"About what? He's not going to talk to us now anyway."

"I'd like to talk to him again. To let him know that Freddy is doing all right."

"If he'll see you you can see him, Kim."

Joyce said, "What I don't understand is why you don't have fingerprints or a strand of hair, something like that. You know, the incriminating evidence that will tell you who is doing these things."

"Fingerprints we've got. That's the problem. Can you imagine how many prints we got from Enid Flaherty's apartment? The vast majority of them are unknown and probably always will be. The car that killed her? Zilch. Where helpful prints might have been found, they were wiped off. I'm not looking for that kind of break. We need something else."

"Like what?"

"A good guess. I've got to go."

After Audrey and Terry had dropped Marge off the night before, they had gone on to have dinner at a Chinese restaurant. They had tea with their meal, two pots of tea. They did not care if they never had another drink.

"And Terry never will," Audrey said musingly. "I haven't had one yet myself."

The conversation? About what you would expect. Reviewing their friendship with Enid and thinking what a raw deal she had had from life. She had been a natural MOMSIE, they were sure of that, and, if she had lived, she would almost certainly have become a member. Of course Freddy had been a problem. Enid insisted on keeping him, just as Marge insisted on keeping her daughter.

"Did you see anyone there?"

"At the Pagoda? No one we knew. I'm not wild about Chinese food but Terry wanted it in the worst way. God, did we have lots of it. It seemed ghoulish having that kind of appetite when we had just buried Enid, but we were both famished. Fried rice, sweet and sour pork, egg rolls, everything." Audrey's expression became sadder. "It was Terry's last meal."

Kim said, "Do you remember the fellow who was at the funeral home? Greg?"

"Jack who became Greg? Sure. He was at the cemetery too. Weird."

"There was another man with him. Did you notice him?"

"At the funeral home?"

"I didn't see him there but he was at the cemetery standing next to Greg."

Audrey took her lower lip between her teeth and thought. "What did he look like?"

"Nondescript, except for his hair."

Kim described the man, and Audrey's head shook back and forth. "That doesn't sound like anyone I know."

"Terry pointed him out to me."

"Who did she say he was?"

"She didn't. Donald Schneider went to pieces then and I never got a chance to ask her. That was why Sister Mary Teresa and I went over there yesterday."

"What's so important about him?"

"Maybe nothing at all. He must have known Enid, and Terry seemed to know him. Why did she point him out to me? It may mean absolutely nothing, but Sister Mary Teresa is even more curious than I am."

Marge had not noticed the man either. She was unaware that Greg had been at graveside. The two women were now ensconced in the house on Walton Street and Kim felt that it was Marge more than Audrey who benefited from the promise of security. Marge's daughter was staying with her father.

It took Kim time and ingenuity to find Greg so she could ask him about the stranger with the odd hair. It should have been easy. Nag Richard until he told her Greg's full name and then go see him.

"I'd rather we go about this without annoying or disturbing the police," Emtee Dempsey said.

"But they already know about him."

"You mean Greg alias Jack? Do they know he attended the funeral?"

Emtee Dempsey's mind was made up and it was Kim's task to locate and talk with Greg without bothering the police. She considered various possibilities, among them calling Jennie Probst. But it was Emtee's reminder that he had been at the funeral that suggested a better way.

There were no bodies in any of the viewing rooms of Philpott's Mortuary and that might have explained the unction with which Kim was met when she was ushered into the funeral director's office by a receptionist whose two hundred pounds made it difficult for her to retain the abject expression that went with the job. Philpott rose from behind his desk, head to one side, shoulders sagged.

"Please be seated," he said lugubriously.

"A few days ago you buried Enid Flaherty."

A flicker of concern momentarily altered Philpott's funereal expression. "Ye-e-e-s."

"I've come to pick up the visitors' book."

Philpott sat back in his chair and placed his long-fingered hands flat on the uncluttered desk. "Indeed."

"You still have it, I hope."

"No-o-o. Dr. Flaherty took it away with him when he settled the account. For whom would you have wanted it, Madam?"

"For her husband," Kim said. "It would have been a great consolation to him."

"But didn't he . . ." Philpott paused. "Isn't he responsible for his wife's death?"

"You haven't been reading the newspapers."

Kim rose. If Dr. Michael Flaherty had the visitors' book she would have to see him in order to find out if Greg had signed his name in full. Philpott came with her to the door, bent forward, moving like a grounded bird. If there were any way at all he could be of help . . .

"It's funny you should ask," Dr. Michael Flaherty said. "The police picked it up this morning."

The office in which they sat did not look like a doctor's office, probably because it was where Dr. Flaherty directed the activities of his several labs. He wore a blue business suit. There were sailing trophies on the shelves behind him.

"Did you look through it?"

"I didn't have time. Besides, I believe I met everyone personally. Are they looking for a substitute for Harry?"

"When will he be released?"

"Not immediately. If he hadn't been arraigned, I think they'd let him go. From what I'm told, it's just a formality now. Thank God."

"Did you know everybody at the funeral?"

"I knew practically no one there."

"There were two men at graveside . . ."

"Boy friends of Enid's, I suppose."

"Terry Stansky pointed them out to me. But she didn't identify them and now . . ."

"You think one of those men murdered her?"

"Apparently the police have the same thought."

"They are in a far better position to pursue it, aren't they?" Dr. Flaherty regarded her as if he were still not sure whose side she was on. Until he knew, he would be distantly polite.

"My brother Richard is a policeman."

"Is that so? Richard Moriarity? He came for the visitors' book. There's your solution. You need only ask your brother."

It was Katherine Senski who got the information for Kim. A *Trib* reporter had taken a glimpse at the visitors' book and had been permitted to photocopy the pages on which people had written their names. There were only three pages and would have been less if the early arrivals had not skipped a line between signatures. It was odd that Dr. Flaherty had wanted the book, since he had not bothered to write his own name in it. Nor had his brothers, if they had even been there. The senior Schneiders too were absent, but Donald had printed his name; it was the most prominent entry on the page. Terry, Marge, Audrey, Joyce, and Kim. There were other women from the neighborhood as well.

Joyce was in the study with Kim and Katherine when they studied the photocopy and she helped them identify all but three names: Gregory Hubert, Hale Ashburling, and Victor Sansfil.

"Gregory Hubert must be Jack."

Katherine Senski hummed. "Not exactly the sort you would imagine hanging around the Tara Beer Hall. He's an accountant with a moderately good firm, unmarried, otherwise of sober life style."

"'Hanging around' is a fair description, is it?" Emtee Dempsey asked.

"He is a not infrequent patron."

Kim said, "The MOMSIES say the same thing. Not that obliquely, of course."

"Has your reporter interviewed him, Katherine?"

"No. But the police have."

"And what did they learn?"

"Your tone implies that there are things he might not have told them."

"Was he asked about the other names on the list?"

"The police already knew that Ashburling is a clerk at Jewels, where Enid shopped."

"Hale," Joyce said. "Of course. I didn't see him at Philpott's, but I know Hale. What's his last name? Ashburling. Wow! I didn't know that."

"Which leaves Victor Sansfil. Did Gregory Hubert know him? Who is he?" Emtee Dempsey opened a drawer of her desk and took out the Chicago telephone directory.

"Don't bother, Sister. He isn't in it. He pays no taxes in Illinois, Wisconsin, or Indiana, and he has no driver's license. Nor does he have a social security number."

"That sounds like the description of someone who does not exist. The name is false?"

"So the police have concluded."

"And Gregory Hubert did not know him?"

"How could he know someone who doesn't exist?"

"The man who wrote this name exists. Perhaps he is the bushy-haired individual to whom Terry Stansky drew Sister Kimberly's attention at the cemetery. I shall assume that he is. Does Gregory Hubert know the man under whatever name? That is what I should like to ask him."

Meaning she would like Kim to ask Gregory Hubert the question for her. But the question was one Kim herself wanted answered. She telephoned Greg at his apartment. He had just come in the door. He intended to play tennis on the courts of the complex in which he lived. Kim would find him there.

Fifty minutes later, Kim sat in an aluminum chair in the shade of a chestnut while Gregory Hubert cooled down from his match. His hair was soaked, as if he had already taken the shower he was headed for. He breathed in great gasps and his complexion was pink. It was difficult to think such exhausting exercise was healthful.

"He wasn't with me," Greg said, shaking his head. He said it a word at a time, gasping in between. "I went there alone."

"He was standing next to you at the cemetery."

"What did he look like?"

Kim described him, concentrating inevitably on the hair.

"Sounds like a rug. I didn't notice him." His breathing was more regular now. "That really socked me, Enid's death. Someone that young, someone you had known. It gets to you. That's why I've decided to get back in shape. And now Terry Stansky. What's going on?"

"The police have talked to you, haven't they?"

"What can I tell them? I met these women at a bar a couple of times; we talked, had a few drinks." He shrugged. "I suppose they figure I went home with them but I didn't. I didn't bring them here either."

Behind him on the clay courts tennis balls bonged back and forth across the nets, versicle and response.

"With Enid it seemed simple because her husband had been threatening her life. But that won't work with Terry Stansky. Her husband is in Saudi Arabia. Maybe it changes the picture on Enid's death too."

He nodded. He took the towel from around his neck and began to rub his head with it.

"So maybe the two murders are connected," Kim said.

He looked at her with red-rimmed eyes. "That's pretty obvious, isn't it?"

"In what way?"

"Well, they're friends. They hang out together. Go to the same places. First one is killed, then the other."

"But what's the motive? And forget Enid's husband."

"Motive? That's old-fashioned. What's the motive for nine-tenths of the violence that goes on in this city?"

"The death of two friends isn't random. You said so yourself."

"They had a common enemy."

"But what could they have done to anyone that would make them candidates for murder? Can you imagine?"

"Look, I'm an accountant. I'm not in the imagining business. But you hang around places like the Tara Beer Hall and you're going to run into a wide spectrum of weird characters. The women you meet there are kinky. They're there to be picked up. A one-night stand." Greg shook his head. He seemed shocked, despite the fact that he too went there. Kim mentioned that.

"No more. I went out of curiosity and then went back a couple times for the same reason. I mean, it's something you have to see to believe, women on the prowl."

"Where are you from originally?"

"Indiana. Goshen, Indiana."

"Isn't that Amish country?"

"And Mennonite."

"I don't suppose there are any Tara Beer Halls in Goshen."

"Are you kidding? I suppose I had to see the place for myself when I heard of the Tara."

Kim returned to the man who had been standing next to Greg in the cemetery, but he could not remember seeing anyone like the person she described. She asked him to recall it step by step, getting out of his car, crossing the grass to the open grave, the whole sequence.

"All I remember is that guy breaking down. Was that her brother?"

"Yes."

"The poor guy."

"Poor Enid too."

"Yeah."

Terry Stansky was waked in a storefront mortuary. In deference to the faith in which she had been raised, a rosary was scheduled, and she would be buried from the parish in which she grew up. Kim had talked to the priest there and invoked the help of Father Raush, who said Mass for them once a week in the chapel of the house on Walton Street.

"She said she wanted to be cremated, Father."

He smiled. With Kim he was relaxed. Sister Mary Teresa's manner made him stammer like a seminarian. "There's no law against it."

"No Church law either?"

"I'll check."

If he did, he forgot to inform the mortician. Audrey and Marge had told him Terry's wish, expressed the day she died, that she be cremated. When the pastor of her girlhood parish heard that, the funeral Mass was off. Kim was furious with Father Raush. He agreed to lead the rosary and offer a memorial Mass within a few days at the Walton Street chapel.

Joyce and Kim went to the closed-casket wake at seven-thirty. The rosary was scheduled for eight. Marge Pollock was there and two old ladies who apparently never missed a wake at the Wippel Mortuary. Father Raush had not yet arrived. If Enid's send-off had been sad, Terry Stansky's was pathetic.

"Her husband wired that he would cover the expense of the funeral, but he won't be here."

"What does he do in Saudi Arabia?"

"Probably has a harem, if you can believe Terry. He's in the Army. I think he trains Saudi soldiers."

Joyce and Marge went on speculating what anyone might be doing in Saudi Arabia; they might have been talking of the moon. Kim went toward the back of the room. The flowers they had sent, together with several other floral offerings, were reinforced with pots of artificial greenery, Wippel's contribution. Kim was almost afraid to look at the visitors' book for fear no one would have signed it. It lay open on a lectern, a small lamp trained on it. Kim picked up the ballpoint pen with Wippel Mortuary stamped on it. There were three entries on the page. Audrey Larson. Margaret Pollock. Victor Sansfil.

Kim scrawled her name, put down the pen, and hurried back to Marge.

"How long have you been here?"

"I came in just before you did."

"Then you must have seen him. He signed his name after yours. A man. What did he look like?"

"The visitors' book? I signed that this afternoon, when Audrey and I stopped by. She couldn't come tonight and didn't want to come alone."

"Was anyone else here?"

"Sure. Mr. Wippel."

"Where is his office?"

Wippel did not open immediately to Kim's knock and when he came to the door he did not fling it wide. He looked out at Kim as if he had just been doing something reprehensible. And then she caught the scent of liquor.

"Did you see a man sign the visitors' book sometime during the afternoon?"

"A man?" Wippel opened the door now and stepped outside. "This afternoon?"

"It could have been this evening, I suppose. Has your door been open since the wake started?"

"It's never locked. During the day, I mean. When there is a body on view."

"But someone could come without your seeing him?"

"That's very unlikely," Wippel said, the lie riding his breath along with the scent of liquor.

Later, while Father Raush led them through the rosary, Kim was distracted by many thoughts. Wippel and Marge were there, but only Joyce and Kim answered the prayers as the priest plowed through the decades of Hail Marys. Victor Sansfil had attended Enid's wake and had come to view the closed coffin containing the mortal remains of Terry Stansky as well. Would he show up at the crematorium tomorrow? It seemed at least possible, perhaps even probable. Joyce nudged her elbow to get her to slow down. Kim could hardly wait to tell Emtee Dempsey what she had found.

The old nun could not quite conceal her own excitement at the news. It was the kind of occurrence that appealed to her sense of mystery.

"Victor Sansfil," she murmured. "The Victor is easy, but what of the surname? Sands fill? *Sans fils?* Childless?"

"Wireless!" Kim cried. "*Télégraphie sans fil.* French for radio."

"Radio winner?" Emtee Dempsey wrinkled her nose in distaste. "That doesn't make any sense."

"What is your guess?"

"Guesses. They are equally meaningless. Let us hope he shows up for the cremation tomorrow. I would go myself but I will not lend a shred of respectability to cremation by my presence. Besides, people might be shocked to see me there."

"That's true," Kim said. "Joyce and I don't matter."

"Not dressed the way you dress."

Touché! More French. Later, in bed, Kim tried other variations on the name someone had twice written in visitors' books. She tried it backward. Slifsnas. Snasslif. Life? Snuffs life? But even as she composed anagrams from the name she became more convinced that her first guess was as good as any. *Sans fil.* Wireless. Radio. But what did that have to do with Enid Flaherty and Terry Stansky?

Six

Several days passed without further developments. In the study of the house on Walton Street the sound of the scratching pen of Sister Mary Teresa was only intermittently heard, and when Kim looked in the old nun was seated motionless at her desk, eyes closed, a frown on her face. She did not want to talk of the murders of Enid Flaherty and Terry Stansky but it was clear she was thinking of little else.

Richard telephoned twice and stopped by once, but he had little to add to what they already knew. Perhaps he was hoping Emtee Dempsey would have an inspired guess. She seemed equally disappointed in him.

"Were there prints in Terry's apartment that matched those in Enid's?"

"Sure. Enid's and Terry's. And those other MOMSIES'."

He did not drop his voice though he knew Marge and Audrey were staying with them still. Marge spent the day helping Joyce around the house while Audrey went off for her shift at Spring-fresh.

"Any common ones you can't identify?"

"No."

After Richard left, Emtee Dempsey lapsed into silence again. Kim went up to her room to study, but half an hour later her phone buzzed. It was Emtee Dempsey.

"When the police first came to Enid's apartment last Tuesday morning, did they look around thoroughly?"

"They looked around."

"Their search was perfunctory?"

"I guess so."

"I do not receive the impression that they have gone back since. The same may be true of Terry Stansky's apartment. Do you still have your key?"

She did, but it would not have mattered if she did not. The MOMSIES, it turned out, each had keys to the apartments of other members of the club. Enid Flaherty had entered into this arrangement. Kim suppressed a sigh. She was content to leave the investigation of the two murders in the hands of the police. Besides, she was woefully behind on her seminar paper. She had skipped the Monday meeting in the hope of finishing it, but she had spent the time she saved at the Newberry on an errand for Emtee Dempsey and that evening Katherine Senski came to report on Raphael Hennessy.

"Raphael? Such a name for a fallen angel?"

"Not really. He's a pillar of his parish. You would be edified by the life he leads, the Tara Beer Hall apart."

Kim was edified and so was Emtee Dempsey, if grudg-ingly. Hennessy was an usher at St. Winifred's, a member of the Holy Name Society, and had long been active in Scouting. It displeased him that his bar had turned into the kind of place it was but there seemed little he could do about it.

"Perhaps if he spent more money on lighting."

"The daytime clientele is much the same, Sister. He does nothing to foster the atmosphere the patrons create. As a matter of fact, he has been thinking of selling the place if he cannot soon change its character."

"He is still positive it was Harry Flaherty who created a fuss at Enid's table?"

"He is positive."

"At two in the morning?"

"Closer to three."

Emtee Dempsey moved her fountain pen from one spot on her desk to another. "Well, it almost certainly does not matter."

Katherine contested that. They must not forget that Harry Flaherty's handkerchief had been found in the car that killed Enid. The police were now inclined to separate the murders of Enid and Terry, seeing Harry as the cause of the first and an unknown assailant as responsible for the second. Kim thought of the stranger with the odd hair who had been present at the cemetery when Enid was buried. If he was taken to be the murderer of Terry Stansky, why had he been at Enid's graveside? She put that question to Katherine Senski.

"He was stalking his victim," Katherine said.

Emtee Dempsey made a derisive noise and that was all. It was clear she would not easily give up her belief that the two murders were connected and that the best way to connect them was by having one murderer, not two.

One afternoon Donald Schneider showed up at the door, wanting to see his nephew. Freddy went off with him to White Sox Park despite the threat of rain and they were back within half an hour in a downpour. Donald, though obviously uncomfortable in the house, stayed until Audrey returned from Springfresh at five-thirty. Then he went back to the Holiday Inn where he was staying. That night Marge, Audrey, Joyce, and Kim played bridge at the kitchen table while Sister Mary

Teresa brooded in her study. Donald had not wished to talk with so obvious a nun as Emtee and Joyce assured him that he need not.

Now Emtee Dempsey wanted Kim to go over Enid Flaherty's apartment with a fine-toothed comb.

"What would I be looking for?"

"I don't know. Remember my watch."

Remember that it had been missing from Enid's apartment or found in Terry's? Kim had suggested that Sister Mary Teresa turn it over to the police in the hope that fingerprints would be found on it, but the old nun scoffed at the idea. She asked Kim to recall the way her brother Richard had pawed the watch as he read the inscription on it. An absence as much as a presence would be the object of Kim's search. Kim could hardly be a good judge of what might be missing from the apartment but that difficulty could be overcome by taking one of the MOM-SIES with her. Marge refused.

"I couldn't. I just couldn't."

Marge was still overwhelmed by the thought that two of her friends were dead, murdered, and the fact that she was staying on Walton Street because of possible danger upset her further. She did not consider the danger imaginary. She was convinced someone was intent on killing her.

"Who?"

"I don't know. That's why it's so terrible."

Since Audrey was at work, the search would have to be postponed until later, after supper, but Kim was unable to study in the interim. Concentration came hard when there were guests in the house and Emtee Dempsey was preoccupied with the murders of Enid and Terry.

Audrey was willing enough to accompany Kim, perhaps spurred by the thought of another evening of bridge in a convent kitchen. Both she and Marge were outspoken in their resolve to change their lives, to quit drinking and frequenting places like the Drumbeat and the Tara Beer Hall. Audrey seemed to see her future stretch before her bleak and dreary. The prospect of making a thorough search of Enid's apartment excited her if only as a distraction from her ascetic resolutions.

"What can we find that the police haven't?" she asked when they were on their way in the VW Bug.

"I haven't the faintest idea. The police may not have made much of a search."

"Well, I'm willing to take a go at it." Audrey was back in jeans for the occasion and Kim wondered how she could move in so tight an outfit.

They began with Enid's apartment and started with her bedroom, and if Audrey found it ghoulish to be going through her friend's things this was offset by a natural curiosity. As Terry had before her, she spent a lot of time in the closet looking through Enid's dresses.

"What will become of all these?"

"Saint Vincent de Paul, I suppose."

"Who's he?"

"It's like Goodwill."

"That seems a shame."

"I imagine you and Marge would be permitted to take some things. That would be up to Harry."

Audrey seemed about to say something but did not. Kim went back to the contents of the drawer in the bedside table. There was a Bible in which Enid had noted the date of her marriage to Harry, the birth of Freddy and his baptism. The names of her parents and grandparents were also given, but the blanks for Harry's were just that — blanks. Perhaps he thought it would be false to put down the names of Flahertys. And there were letters, lots of them, all with a Baraboo postmark. For the most part they were from Mrs. Schneider, but there were several from Donald as well and the burden of them all was the same. Kim had not realized the depth of the Schneiders' aversion to Catholicism. Enid was warned in Biblical tones that she must draw no nearer to the Whore of Babylon than she already was. The Reverend Skillen was quoted at length, his fiery condemnations of the Church of Rome of a kind seldom heard in this ecumenical age. Donald easily vied with the preacher in his view of the danger Enid was running.

> Dear Sis,
>
> We prayed for you again in church last night. Your husband is already lost but there is hope for you and the boy. You know what this is doing to Mom. She would rather see you dead than join your husband's so-called religion. Sin is death, but to take that step would be worse than sin, worse than death. God is not mocked.

That sort of thing went on for pages, and Kim read with wonderment this portrayal of her faith. Had she ever considered other denominations in this way? Emtee Dempsey was wont to watch television evangelists and was quick to stifle the amusement Joyce expressed. "All Christians are one," was her final word on the subject. To guarded remarks about excess, she replied that to many the apostles and saints had seemed fanatics. For so thorough a Catholic as Emtee Dempsey this was tolerance indeed. There was little tolerance evident in the letters Enid received from Baraboo. Kim marveled at the fact that the Schneiders had found it possible to spend even a brief time at the house on Walton Street or to agree that their grandson should remain there, if only temporarily. But how could they have coped with him in Baraboo? Donald's concern about his nephew now took on another aspect and Kim wondered if it had been Terry's funeral or Freddy that explained his second trip from Baraboo. But then, according to his mother, Donald visited Chicago from time to time. Had he contacted Enid on those visits? The answer to that was in the letters. He referred to telephone conversations and lamented the fact that she refused to see him and discuss the condition of her soul. The letters made Kim uneasy and she put them back in the drawer.

"Find anything?" Audrey asked.

"Just letters from home.

"Oh God. Are they as bad as Enid said?"

"What did she say?"

Audrey hesitated. "I guess they are pretty religious."

"Was Enid?"

"Not that I ever noticed."

Audrey was holding against her a knit dress that was too small in size and far too long in the skirt for her. She stooped to look in the mirror over the dresser.

"Isn't this gorgeous?"

Kim said nothing. Audrey would fit more comfortably into Emtee Dempsey's habit than into a dress of Enid's. Reluctantly Audrey returned the dress to the closet and went to the kitchen to see if there was coffee. But when she came back she carried a bottle of beer.

"Want one?"

"No thanks."

"Beer doesn't count as drinking," Audrey said, as if Kim had chided her for backsliding on her resolution not to drink.

"I don't like the taste."

That wasn't quite true, but she was reminded of the night in the Tara Beer Hall when she had drunk a bottle of beer just because it cost three dollars. Would Raphael Hennessy justify the price as an effort to discourage custom? They went on to the living room where they sat while Audrey drank her beer. She looked around the room.

"I saw her body and I still can't believe she's dead. This place brings her back—the rooms, the clothes."

The beer seemed to promote sentimentality and, when Audrey finished it and went for another, commenting on how weird it felt drinking beer Enid would have bought on the assumption she herself would drink it, she began to talk aimlessly. Or apparently aimlessly. The mystery of Emtee Dempsey's watch was solved as Audrey babbled.

"In the bedroom you said Marge and I should take something of Enid's, for a remembrance, and I said nothing, remember? The reason was we already had. Terry and Marge and I. We had keys, of course, and we thought we should take some small thing to remember Enid by and we came here and I took a necklace and Marge a silk scarf, but Terry wanted to take that watch and we told her it was too expensive and besides none of us had ever seen Enid with it — Terry found it in Freddy's bedroom — but she insisted. Then there was a sound at the door and we got the hell out, leaving by the back door and running up to Terry's apartment, and it was you and your brother, as we found out when Terry decided to creep down and see who was here. Well, you caught her, and Marge and I were listening on the stairs, petrified, but anyway Terry took the watch and that is why it was found in her apartment."

"She didn't get to keep it long."

"No." Audrey sipped her beer and looked at Kim. "It's awful to say, but I was almost relieved when Terry was killed."

"What do you mean?"

"I couldn't ever tell Marge this, she'd never forgive me, I don't know if I can tell you — after all, you're a nun."

"Tell me."

"I don't know. I was letting down the side. And I know what you'll think."

"Of what?"

Audrey put down her beer and lit one of her odd cigar-colored cigarettes. "You remember I told you I had that date with Harry Flaherty?"

"I remember."

"Like I said, he told me about his wife and all. Enid. What I didn't say is he knew I knew Enid. Also, I had another date with him."

"When?"

"You're going to think I'm awful."

"Please tell me, Audrey."

"It was the night Enid was killed! Harry was with me, at my place. It's awful how you can be fascinated by a man when you know so many bad things about him. He wasn't all bad, though. He's an orphan, did you know that? That really touched me. What is that like, knowing your parents aren't your parents, wondering who your real parents are? That's got to disturb a person. And he is good-looking. Still and all, it was a dirty trick to play on Enid and I knew it. But if I'd seen him once, another time was hardly worse. Harry telephoned and I said sure, come over, and he did and we had a few drinks and, well..."

It was hard to say what Audrey's pleading look expected by way of a reply.

"That was a week ago Monday?"

Audrey nodded, her head bobbing up and down, as if Kim had made a good guess in Charades.

"Monday night," she said through a puff of smoke. "And Tuesday morning."

"When did he leave?"

"I'm not sure." Audrey looked away, one elbow cupped in her hand, the cigarette held between two pudgy fingers. A woman of the world. "I know it was after two. I was so sleepy and after a few drinks and..." Again that pleading look. Kim ignored it.

"How could you keep quiet about that?"

"Think about it! Here I was, the big MOMSIE, agreeing with Enid about what a rat she'd married, and I'm sleeping with him the night she gets killed. I've been living in dread that Harry will tell them where he was and it'll be in all the papers and Marge and Terry would never speak to me again and I wouldn't blame them. Why hasn't Harry told them where he was? I'm his alibi!"

"Not if he left your place when you think he did."

"Even so. If he says he spent the whole night with me how can I deny it?"

"By telling the truth."

"Sure. The truth. But then Terry was killed and I said, it's awful, but I was really relieved. I mean, Harry couldn't have killed her, could he?"

"That doesn't mean he didn't kill Enid."

"But I thought..."

Kim let it go. She knew what Audrey thought. Whoever killed Enid killed Terry, and Harry was in jail when Terry was killed. The possibility that that argument did not work upset Audrey.

"I just don't believe he could leave me and go out and kill Enid. I do not believe that."

"I wish we knew who that man was at Enid's burial."

"Jack? Greg?"

"No, the other one. The one with the funny hair."

"He could have been anyone."

He had not been a cop. Richard assured her of that, even while smiling at her description of the man's hair. He too thought it was a wig, but it was pretty clear he thought Kim was imagining things.

"Was he carrying a shovel?"

"Funny."

"Kim, the mysterious stranger is the stuff of fiction."

Richard had not been amused when Emtee Dempsey reacted in a similar way to his suggestion that Terry had been killed by an unknown assailant, her death having nothing to do with Enid's.

Kim and Audrey resumed their search of the apartment. Audrey was less help after the two beers. Thank God there were no more in the refrigerator. Audrey would certainly have drunk all that was there. She already had. There was a book with numbers in it by the phone in the living room and Kim slipped it into her purse. It was late and she suggested they call it a night.

Emtee Dempsey listened to Kim's report of the search but it was the explanation of Terry's having her watch and Audrey's confession that Harry Flaherty had spent part of that fateful Monday night in her bed that interested the old nun.

"She is unsure when he left?"

"She says it was after two or around two."

"On what basis?"

"Do you want to talk with her about it?"

A look of distaste appeared on Emtee Dempsey's face. "Only as a last resort. I hope Harry Flaherty will not need her testimony. If he does, she will have to speak out."

"That doesn't change Hennessy's testimony that he saw Harry in the Tara Beer Hall just before the killing."

"It would confuse the jury."

"It confuses me."

"Nonsense. Harry Flaherty did not kill his wife. I do not see any great significance in the quarrel with Enid at the bar."

"What makes you so sure?"

"My conviction that the two deaths are related. I simply do not believe in the kind of coincidence the police seem comfortable with. In the morning, stop by the Holiday Inn and see how long Donald Schneider has been registered there."

"What for?"

"If they want to know why you're asking, mention Katherine Senski's name."

"I am not going to pretend I am a reporter."

Emtee Dempsey's eyebrows shot up. "Did I suggest that you should?"

"Why else would I mention Katherine?"

"Because she would be as curious as I am."

"And it would appear that I am with the *Tribune*."

"You are not responsible for the inferences people make when you utter perfectly innocuous remarks."

"That is devious and you know it."

"It is indirect but not devious. Why would they respond

to a reporter who made such queries? Because, the theory goes, the public has a right to know. Very well. You are a member of the public. Katherine, or any reporter, is actually acting as your lieutenant in making such inquiries. You are simply eliminating the middleman and acting for yourself."

"Then I need not mention Katherine."

"I would advise you to do so. We cannot rely on a room clerk's having a logical mind."

Sister Mary Teresa could make Kim's head spin with such justifications for doing whatever she wanted to do. Kim knew there was a fallacy lurking in Emtee Dempsey's reasoning but she was not sure what it was. What she did know was that she would not pretend to be a reporter.

After Mass and breakfast the following day, a Thursday, Kim drove to the Holiday Inn in a rainstorm. She dashed from the parking lot to the entrance and when she approached the desk, carrying only her shoulder bag, the girl behind the desk seemed undecided whether to offer her a registration card. The irises of the girl's eyes suggested she was wearing contact lenses. Her hair-do, reminiscent of a coiled steel scouring pad, contributed to her startled expression.

"Is Mr. Donald Schneider registered here?"

"May I ask why you want to know?"

"I am looking after his nephew. He's staying with me."

This satisfied the girl. So much for Emtee Dempsey's foolishness about posing as a reporter. The truth was all one needed, the unvarnished truth. Kim looked forward to telling the old nun how easy it was.

"He checked out this morning."

"Are you sure?"

God knew what experiences prompted the lidded look the girl gave her. "I'm sure."

"The Donald Schneider from Baraboo who registered on Monday?"

"No, not Monday. Mr. Schneider has been with us a week."

"Since last Thursday?"

"A week ago. Yes.

"Thank you."

Since last Thursday? The feeling of triumph she had felt at the thought of explaining to Sister Mary Teresa the strength of the simple truth dissipated. What had prompted Emtee Dempsey's curiosity about Donald's stay at the Holiday Inn? It had to be what Kim had said about his letters to Enid, but what a stab in the dark. If it was a stab in the dark. Good Lord! If Donald had been staying at the Holiday Inn since last Thursday he had been in Chicago when Terry Stansky was killed.

In the parking lot of the motel Kim sat behind the wheel of the VW, her hands gripping it, staring at the nails of her outthrust thumbs. Life was a vehicle one steered, but only in part; the earth on which the vehicle moves itself moves. What we intend is only part of what we do. Large thoughts, morning thoughts, thoughts brought on by a possibility she had not dreamed of, but now that possibility asserted itself with all the authority of the truth. Each day, in the chapel of the house on Walton Street, Kim spent an hour in meditation, beginning with carefully organized points for consideration, but soon, by distraction or sometimes, it seemed, by inspiration, her mind was swept downward into the depths of herself and hidden strengths and weaknesses were revealed. It was fine to think of life as a challenge to be met, of character as something constructed according to a thought-out plan, but is that ever the way it really is? Hunches, intuitions, ideas without willed origin, could set one on an unknown path that was somehow familiar. Is this how Emtee Dempsey had hit upon the notion of checking the register of the Holiday Inn?

Kim turned the ignition key. She would take what she had found back to Sister Mary Teresa and let her handle it. This was more than Kim cared to think about. She backed out of her parking space and headed for the street, trying to make of her mind the blankest of blanks.

"You had better inform the police," Emtee Dempsey said after spending a moment absorbing the information Kim brought. "Tell them about the letters too."

"What does it mean?"

"I don't know. We will leave that to the police to determine."

"That doesn't sound like you."

"Two women have been murdered. The police think others are in danger."

Richard, when she reached him, listened, making little noises over the line as he did, but whether they were meant to express gratitude or annoyance Kim could not tell.

"He checked out of the Holiday Inn?"

"Just this morning."

"Okay. We'll look into it."

"You're welcome."

"Sure. Thanks."

"Will you let me know what you find out?"

There was a pause. "Okay. Meanwhile, go back to saying prayers, will you, please?"

"We've never stopped."

"Just say them at home for a change. How did you get into the Flaherty apartment?"

He knew how. "Richard, can't you just say thanks and let it go at that?"

When she had put down the phone, she said to Sister Mary Teresa, "He asked for our prayers."

No response. Emtee Dempsey had not been following Kim's side of the conversation. She was turning the pages of the little telephone book Kim had brought from Enid's living room. There were not many entries in the book and none that addressed the old nun's curiosity. She closed the book and stared at its cover.

"There is a number here but no indication whose it is." Her pudgy finger pointed to some penciled digits on the cover. "Why don't you dial it and see who answers?"

She turned the book around and pushed it across the desk to Kim. 002-4231. Kim made a face and dialed the number. It was answered on the second ring.

"WXYZ, good morning."

"WXYZ?"

"That's right. Good morning."

"Did the Sox win last night?"

"I'll put you through to Sports. Please hold."

A click and then a soft flow of Muzak in her ear. Kim put down the phone. Emtee Dempsey looked up at her.

"A television station?"

"Radio."

"Hmmm. Perhaps you should return this to her apartment. Unless you want to give it to the police."

But Kim's mind was racing. Radio. Victor Sansfil. Wireless. There had to be a connection, but what was it? Sister Mary Teresa did not believe in coincidence where the two murders were concerned. Kim did not believe there was no connection between the enigmatic entry in those visitors' books and the number of WXYZ Enid Flaherty had scrawled on the cover of her little book of telephone numbers. There was no doubt she had written the number. Kim compared it with those inside and they were by the same hand.

"What is it?" Emtee Dempsey asked.

"Radio. WXYZ. Remember the name in the visitors' books?"

"Ah. What does it mean?"

"I wish I knew."

Emtee Dempsey was equally mystified and seemed torn between regarding it as significant or insignificant. For the time

* *127* *

being there was the far more promising lead of Donald Schneider but, since she had conceded the police must pursue that, she urged Kim to seek a connection between the unknown mourner and the radio station number on the cover of Enid Flaherty's book.

"By which I mean, forget it. The mind has mountains, Sister Kimberly, and they are best scaled inadvertently. Recollection is not reminiscence."

There was more, allusions to Aristotle but not to Freud, on the mysteries of human memory. Sometimes reminiscence led to recollection, of course, but this seldom happened when all one had was the teasing conviction that there was something hidden in the past that would link two notions presently before the mind. Kim was not reluctant to escape the lecture and go down the hall to the kitchen for a cup of coffee with Joyce.

Freddy was outside and Marge was seated at the table, the morning paper open to the crossword puzzle, a mug of coffee within reach.

"What's a four-letter word for event?"

"No four-letter words in my kitchen," Joyce said, revving her mixer.

The radio on the counter, volume low, provided unheeded background music. Marge pushed the paper away. "I feel like such a freeloader. And I'm bored. No offense, Joyce. Why do I have to stay here if Audrey can go to work?"

"The police think she's safe in a public place."

"It made sense when they thought it was Harry. I mean, he had some kind of reason to kill Enid, or at least he thought he did. Now it's just spooky."

It would have been unwise to tell Marge about Donald Schneider. The woman was frightened enough as it was, her eyes staring at a world she no longer understood. Two of her friends had been murdered within days of each other, she was stashed in a convent for an indefinite period and not even Joyce and the crossword puzzle could take her mind from that. Kim wondered how Marge spent the day when she was home.

Kim considered returning Enid's telephone directory to her apartment rather than give it to Richard. If the number on its cover meant anything, she did not know what it was and all she was likely to get for her pains was a scolding, something she could do without. Besides, the visitors' books from Philpott's and Wippel's were in their possession. Unless Dr. Flaherty had told Richard Kim had asked about the book from Philpott's, he might not know of the odd entry that seemed to link the man with the funny hair and WXYZ. But, they had advantage enough over Richard without depriving him of Enid's book of phone numbers.

Marge was glad to give Kim her key to Terry's apartment though she seemed to dread being asked to go along. Kim, since she planned to continue to Northwestern, had no desire to take Marge with her.

What is emptier than an empty apartment, particularly a strange one? Standing in Enid's living room, Kim was keenly reminded of that fateful Monday evening when she had seen Enid off on her last night of fun. She put the telephone book on the table and wandered through the apartment. Later, upstairs in Terry's apartment, a neater brighter place than Enid's, Kim turned on the radio to drive away some of the emptiness. And that is when the penny dropped.

The sound of country-Western music died away and a memorable voice was heard.

"Bud Drabble, ladies and gentlemen. During this half-hour we will be featuring 'Air Affair' and let me tell you we have some very interesting prospects for you today. So stay tuned and, who knows, you may meet the man or woman of your dreams. And now for these commercial messages."

Kim snapped off the radio and stood still. "Air Affair."

Radio. Sansfil. It all fell into place. That was the program Enid listened to. The scribbled number suggested that Enid had called WXYZ. Kim turned on the radio again, pulled up a stool, and listened carefully.

Listeners wishing to contact the men and women who advertised their preferences for a date were asked to call the studio number. Apparently WXYZ acted as matchmaker. The studio would have to know the identities both of those who were interviewed on the air and of those who called in response. A man named Edgar was being interviewed by Bud Drabble.

"Okay, Edgar, you like to bowl and your idea of a nice woman is one who likes the outdoors, hunting, fishing, right?"

"I'll bait her hook, Bud. She doesn't have to worry about that."

"Aha. Gallantry is not dead. How serious are you likely to be with a woman?"

"That depends."

"On how affectionate she is?"

"I like a warm woman, yes."

Again Kim turned off the radio. When she left the apartment, her destination was not the Northwestern campus but the house on Walton Street.

"You should have told me of that program before," Emtee Dempsey said grumpily. "That might have saved us time."

"It didn't seem important."

"Now the question is how to proceed. Where is WXYZ located?"

"On the near North Side."

"Is the program on the air now?"

Kim looked at her watch. It was after one-thirty. "It's just ended."

"Then Mr. Drabble should still be there. How do you intend to proceed?"

"I don't intend to proceed at all. They're not likely to get out their records for me. Why should they?"

Emtee Dempsey closed her eyes briefly. "Because you are a graduate student interested in 'Air Affair.' You would like to do research on the kind of people who participate in it. Your inquiries will be tactful and confidential. Your work will be facilitated if the station, particularly Mr. Drabble, will put you in touch with the participants and assure them yours is a scientific study, not merely prying curiosity."

"Sister Mary Teresa, I am a graduate student in history, not in sociology."

"You are also my research assistant. It is I who have conceived an interest in 'Air Affair' and must have information on it. The contrast with medieval practices has piqued my interest. You shall be my eyes and ears, my arms and legs. It is all quite straightforward."

Kim might have told her that all her misleading obliquity had been unnecessary at the Holiday Inn, but this would have suggested she herself thought a simple direct approach would open the records of "Air Affair" to her. She did not believe that for a moment. Emtee Dempsey was pulling the telephone toward her.

"What are you doing?"

"I am going to call Mr. Drabble, identify myself and my interests, and ask when he will be able to speak with you."

"It won't work."

"Do you have a better idea?"

"No."

"Neither do I."

Emtee Dempsey picked up the receiver, thought for a moment, and began to dial. She sat back in her chair, the telephone pressed to her starched headdress, humming as she waited.

"Good afternoon. This is Dr. Dempsey. I would like to speak to Mr. Drabble, please. No, he won't know me. You may tell him that I am a professor emerita of history, that I know his program, and should like to speak with him about it. I will be brief. Yes, I'll wait."

She did not look at Kim. The toneless humming resumed.

"Mr. Drabble? Dr. Mary Teresa Dempsey. No, not a medical doctor. I am a professor emerita of history, a scholar whose work lies in the Middle Ages. Your program has prompted an idea and I wonder if you would help me pursue it. It concerns your fascinating feature 'Air Affair.' No, I do not wish to contact someone. My interests are purely scientific. Let me explain briefly."

The explanation was an unctuous version of the approach she had outlined to Kim. Despite herself, Kim thought it sounded persuasively straightforward. The recurrence of the word "scientific" was not accidental, needless to say. Few could resist a claim to disinterested objective inquiry. Bud Drabble was not among those few.

"Excellent, Mr. Drabble. I am an elderly woman and make use of a research assistant. Would you be willing to speak to her? Kimberly Moriarity. Fine. When would be least inconvenient to you? Tomorrow morning? You are most cooperative. Very well, my research assistant will call on you then. Thank you. Yes. Have a good day yourself."

Emtee Dempsey replaced the receiver without any outward sign of triumph.

"You followed that? What I want to know are the mechanics of the program and what kind of records are kept. Needless to say, you will make no mention of Enid Flaherty until and unless it is necessary. Mr. Drabble is no fool and we do not want to provide him a temptation to broadcast our speculation prematurely. Do you have any questions?"

"Just one. How is 'Air Affair' related to the Middle Ages?"

"A good question. But methodologically unhelpful. There are moments in research when the free play of mind and imagination are necessary. Have you finished Barbara Tuchman's book?"

"Yes."

"*A Distant Mirror*. Mention it to Mr. Drabble. He may have heard of it, though I doubt it. Impress upon him the interest parallels between earlier times and our own currently have for historians."

Kim rose. She wanted to get out of the study before Emtee Dempsey convinced her this visit to WXYZ was indeed connected to the book the old nun was writing.

Seven

WXYZ was a warren of small crowded rooms on the third floor of an old building. An aerial photograph of Chicago in the reception room might have been meant to give a sense of space, but the effect on Kim was that, viewed from a celestial perspective, this place was infinitesimal indeed. The receptionist, an indecisive blonde with a bad complexion, was walled off from visitors and looked out at Kim through a yellowing window in which a brass speaker was embedded. Her smile did not negate the defensive expression in her pale gray eyes nor did Kim's identification of herself bring the warmth of recognition.

"Is Mr. Drabble expecting you?"

"Yes, he is."

The girl picked up a long filtered cigarette from a tray in which the dead ends of a dozen predecessors lay among their ashes, took a deep drag, and picked up the phone.

"Kimberly Moriarity is here. She says you're expecting her."

It was difficult to connect this girl with the bright voice that wished callers to WXYZ a good day. She listened, nodded, put down the phone.

"Come on in."

A buzzer sounded and the girl indicated that Kim was to come through the closed door to her left. Inside, the room in which the receptionist sat behind her aged window looked even smaller, as if the glass had magnified it. She remained seated. Speaking around the bobbing cigarette now between her lips, she said, "Just keep going down the hallway. He's in Studio A."

To the right of the hallway was a series of small offices, for the most part empty. A harried man hammering at a typewriter looked up as Kim went by one office. On her left was a blank wall relieved farther along by a plate-glass window that reminded Kim of the maternity ward in a hospital. The green light was on over the door of Studio A. There did not seem to be any Studio B. Before knocking, Kim caught a glimpse of a corpulent man surrounded by equipment, a desk, tables stacked with papers. He did not look out at her. She knocked and a familiar voice bade her come in.

The impression that she had come into a fire hazard increased when she was in Studio A. It was a room perhaps nine feet square, with acoustical walls and ceiling. No windows, far too much furniture covered with far too much paper, and Bud Drabble. To his left was a turnstile and a long-necked microphone. He swung toward her in the chair that gave him access to everything without rising and peered at her from pouchy eyes. He gave a general appearance of hairiness: bushy brows, a mustache, and locks covering his ears.

"Mr. Drabble?"

"Bud."

"Dr. Dempsey telephoned you yesterday. I am her assistant..."

"Kimberly Moriarity." He read from a slip of paper he plucked from the desk to his right. "Have a seat. Just put that stuff anywhere."

The folding chair was stacked with magazines, newspapers, and, on the bottom, the Chicago telephone directory.

"I wondered where that was," Drabble said, taking the directory from her. "Tell me. Who the hell is Dr. Dempsey?"

"Didn't she say why she called?"

"You tell me."

"Well, she is a well-known scholar, an historian. She taught history for many years at Martha and Mary College west of the city."

"Never heard of it."

"It no longer exists."

Drabble stubbed out his cigarette and immediately took another from the package in his shirt pocket. His jacket was draped over the back of his chair and he was shoeless. His lighter leaped into flame and he added to the smoke in the airless little room. The Surgeon General as well as the Fire Inspector would have had things to say about this place.

"What kind of college was it?"

"Liberal arts. For women. I'm an alumna of the college."

Drabble's mustache drooped at the corners of his mouth, giving him a perpetually sad expression. Kim was having difficulty matching this Buddha-like figure with the chuckling matchmaker on "Air Affair."

"She said her interest is the Middle Ages. I'm not that old."

Kim realized that he was laughing. The chair she sat in did not inspire confidence; she had the feeling that at any moment it would collapse.

"She got this idea that things she is working on in the twelfth century could be interestingly compared with your program."

"Did they have disc jockeys back then?" The coughing sound broke out again.

Kim gave a reasonable facsimile of the argument Emtee Dempsey had developed for Drabble on the phone and he nodded as if he found it plausible. The truth is that it did have an aspect of plausibility about it. At least it seemed to, now that Kim had gotten used to it.

"So what do you want to know?"

"Whatever you can tell me. Dr. Dempsey is fascinated by the whole idea of 'Air Affair.'"

"How old is she?"

"In her seventies. Why?"

"Just a thought. Is she married?"

"No."

"The reason I ask, people sometimes give the damndest reasons why they want to be on the program. You wouldn't believe it." He flicked ashes at the ashtray and missed. He looked sharply at Kim. "There really is a Dr. Dempsey, isn't there?"

"Look her up in *Who's Who*."

"I'll take your word for it. Okay. 'Air Affair.' The idea came to me one day when a woman called while I was on the air, between records. She was drunk, I think, and she wanted to know where a girl could go in Chicago to find a decent man. I kept her on the line and talked to her while I had records on and then, on the spur of the moment, I mentioned her predicament on the air. The response was tremendous. Guys who wanted to meet her. Gals with the same problem. Whitney was in here like a flash, we talked it over for a day or two, and 'Air Affair' was born." He dragged on his cigarette, looking satisfied; he might have been Sir Thomas Fleming discovering the curative effects of mold.

"Who is Whitney?"

"The station manager. Would you believe there was opposition? Shearing, in charge of advertising, tried to put the kibosh on it. Whitney overrode him, though it was touch and go for a while. Now it is the single biggest thing we put out."

"How exactly does it work?"

"What's to work? A gal calls in, I chat with her a bit; if she sounds all right we tape a spot and it goes on the air."

"Don't you ever meet them?"

"Now you sound like my wife. No. It's all done by phone. For all I know, they look like dogs. I accept their descriptions of themselves."

"And those who call in wanting to meet her?"

"Same thing. I never see them."

"And everything is done through the studio telephone number?"

"You bet your booties. On advice of counsel. Sondergaard was another foe of the idea. He's the station's attorney. He predicted all kinds of legal problems, everything from needing a special license to being sued for pandering." Drabble shook his head. They laughed at Edison. He put out his cigarette. His hand fluttered to his shirt pocket but he stopped it en route.

"Do you keep records of the people who call in?"

"Oh, sure. We have them. Sondergaard insisted on that."

"Then you would have the telephone numbers of those who go on the air as well as those of the men who want to contact them?"

"Or women. Both men and women go on the air."

"I know. So you could find what woman contacted what man and vice versa?"

"That's right."

Kim could see why Shearing and Sondergaard had had reservations about the idea. There seemed no way of telling what kind of men might wish to contact a woman. For that matter, what was to prevent a prostitute from appearing on the program? She put that question to Drabble.

"I thought you've listened to the program."

"I have."

"Okay. Then you know we're not dealing here with what you would call the cream of society. Imagine, a woman going on the air saying she wants to meet a guy, any guy. And most of them are willing to say the guy won't be wasting his time. A prostitute's only interest in 'Air Affair' would be to boycott it. She's getting all this amateur competition."

"What about the men? For all you know, some psychopath could call in."

Drabble did light another cigarette now. His eyes narrowed as his smile pushed the pouches up under them. "What's this got to do with the Middle Ages?"

"That's what I'm trying to find out."

He shook his head. "I think I *will* look up Dempsey in *Who's Who*. This sounds more far out all the time." He picked up his phone and punched a button.

"Irene, we got a copy of *Who's Who* out there?" He listened, then turned to Kim. "We've got last year's."

"She's in it."

"Irene, bring it back here, will ya?"

He smoked meditatively while he waited, studying Kim the while. In a minute the door opened and the receptionist came in toting two large red volumes. She looked around for a place to put them.

Kim said, "Give me Volume One."

She opened it, found the page, and handed the book to Drabble. Cigarette in his mouth, he skimmed the entry. He slammed the book shut and handed it to Irene. She leaned over so he could put it atop the volume she still carried.

"You're welcome," Irene said, letting the door hiss shut behind her.

"It still sounds phony to me," Drabble said.

"It is far-fetched, certainly, but Dr. Dempsey is like that."

"You say she's in her seventies?"

"You just read her entry."

"Yeah. What's the Order of Martha and Mary?"

"The order that ran the college she taught in."

"Then she's a nun?"

Emtee Dempsey might have been able to think of a way to parry that question but Kim could not. What difference did it make anyway? Kim told Bud Drabble that, yes, Dr. Mary Teresa Dempsey was a nun.

"What's with the doctor business."

"She's that too. Ph.D."

By now Drabble had noticed the silver cross pinned to Kim's lapel. He said, "You're one too, aren't you?"

"Yes."

"A couple nuns interested in 'Air Affair.'" He shook his head. "I don't believe it. This has nothing to do with the Middle Ages, has it?"

"I told you Sister Mary Teresa's reasons for being interested in your program. She told you herself."

The cigarette Drabble dragged on was scarcely an inch long. "I think I'm beginning to get it. Which one are you interested in?"

"I beg your pardon."

"Come on, give me some credit. You're a nun. You're worried about someone who called 'Air Affair.' Was it someone I had on the air?"

"I don't know. Maybe she just tried to contact a man who was." How welcome it was to tell the simple truth. Drabble, pleased to have his suspicions confirmed, did not crow about it.

"What's her phone number?"

Kim had to look up Enid Flaherty's number and, when she had it, Drabble picked up his phone and punched a different button.

"Zip? Bud. Could I have the 'Air Affair' records, please. Yeah. Studio A."

He put down the phone. "Shearing."

The advertising manager of WXYZ knocked before entering Studio A. He was a small bald man of immaculate appearance whose nose wrinkled in disapproval when he came into the smoke-filled room. His hands were empty and he looked intently at Kim.

Drabble said, "Where are the records?"

"Irene said you had someone with you."

"That's why I want the records. This is Kimberly Moriarity. Sister Kimberly," Drabble added, as if it were a punchline.

Shearing, already erect, straightened more. "I'm Zip Shearing, Sister. Are *you* interested in 'Air Affair?'"

"Indirectly, yes."

"Could you tell me why?"

"Zip, for God's sake, cut it out. You're not in charge here. Where the hell are those records?"

Shearing ignored the announcer. "It is an appalling program. I don't care how much revenue it brings in. This has always been a classy station. Things started going downhill when we let Bud talk us into airing country music."

"It's put bread on your table. And so has 'Air Affair.'"

"Man does not live by bread alone."

"It's put meat on your table too."

"When I came here we played classical music exclusively." Shearing addressed himself to Kim. "Our accounts were modest but they represented some of the most prominent business concerns in Chicago. Now..."

"Now we're making money."

"Sister, I can't tell you how ashamed I am that 'Air Affair' goes out on the call letters of WXYZ."

"I can understand that," Kim said. "But I really would appreciate seeing those records."

Shearing's eyes were set very close together and now seemed to cross in surprise. "Whatever for?"

"Sister Kimberly is the research assistant of Dr. Mary

Teresa Dempsey, the famous historian," Drabble said smoothly. "I just looked her up in *Who's Who*. Fantastic credentials. She's doing some sort of book on the Middle Ages and she thinks 'Air Affair' may have some kind of hook-up with earlier times. Isn't that about it, Sister?"

Kim was reluctant to go back to that fabrication now that she and Drabble were on the solider footing of truth. She looked noncommittal. It did not matter. Shearing was shaking his head vigorously.

"Absolutely not. We assure those people of confidentiality. You can understand that, Sister. Why, it would be like . . ." His eyes lifted in search of a simile and then he had it. "Like breaking the seal of the confessional."

"I didn't know they locked them." It was difficult to know if Drabble was being facetious. Shearing ignored him.

"Bud can tell you all about the feature without divulging confidential information."

Drabble looked at Kim to see if she wanted to try a more truthful approach. She doubted that the truth would fare any better than fiction with Shearing. She stood. Emtee Dempsey could not really blame her for this failure. But Drabble was unwilling to let her go.

"Sit down, Sister. Okay, Zip. Truth time. The fact is that the good Sister has religious reasons for wanting to see those records. One of her flock might be involved."

"Her flock?" Shearing looked impatiently at Drabble. "Nuns do not have flocks, Bud."

"A manner of speaking. Someone they're concerned about. What the hell's the difference? You're not jeopardizing anyone. You may be helping Sister Kimberly to help them."

"Is that true, Sister?"

"Yes." It was close enough, at any rate.

Shearing thought about it. "Even so, I cannot act on my own authority. I will have to consult the station manager and our attorney."

"I don't want to cause a lot of trouble."

"I should add that I am not at all optimistic that Mr. Whitney and Mr. Sondergaard will let you see those records."

It was the memory of Enid Flaherty setting out on her doomed night of fun that stopped Kim from leaving. Enid had listened to that silly program. And there was the mysterious Victor Sansfil.

"Does either of you know a Victor Sansfil?" she asked.

"We do not deal in names," Shearing said quickly. "The names used on the air are fictitious."

"Is Sansfil the one you're worried about?" Drabble asked.

"No." She inhaled. "I am concerned about Enid Flaherty."

"Would you spell that?" Shearing asked, taking a pen from the inside pocket of his suit coat. Kim obliged. She felt she had entered Wonderland but it was her own fault. She had botched the visit and prolonging it would only make things worse. Shearing wanted to know where she could be reached and Kim told him, dreading the thought of a phone call to the house on Walton Street that would make her failure even more obvious.

Shearing held the door for her, indicating that he was all in favor of her going. Kim thanked Bud Drabble. He shrugged and dragged on yet another cigarette. "Sorry, Sister. I would have liked to help you in your scholarly endeavors, but you see my problem."

Shearing pulled the door shut after them and walked with Kim toward the reception area. A man even more prim than Shearing came to the door of one of the offices.

"Can I be of help, Mr. Shearing?"

"No, Charles. Thank you."

Charles's baldness, like Shearing's, seemed an effort to make up for the hirsute vulgarity of Bud Drabble. The young man's eyes flickered from Kim to Shearing and back.

He turned on his heel and retreated to his typewriter.

"Charles does scripts."

Shearing went down to street floor with Kim and walked her out to her car. Sunlight was trying to work its way down through the skyline to the narrow drab street.

Shearing said, "I live in dread that some journalist will do a piece on 'Air Affair.' It's bad enough that we do it, but our old-line advertisers are probably not aware of it." Shearing looked up and down the street as if hordes of reporters and photographers might soon descend upon WXYZ, intent on having the time of their lives with the station that sullied the ozone with its radio dating game.

"Good-by, Mr. Shearing."

"I'll talk to Whitney and Sondergaard." He might have been a parent responding to a child's request with "We'll see."

Kim reported on her visit to WXYZ before they went in to lunch and, on their way to the dining room in response to Joyce's call, Emtee Dempsey said not to bring the matter up at the meal. Marge and Freddy and Joyce chattered inconsequentially, but Emtee Dempsey, distracted, ate her omelet as if she were a million miles away, digesting Kim's story of her morning along with lunch.

Another luncheon, at the Chicago Athletic Club, was devoted to a discussion of Kim's visit to WXYZ, as they learned at two o'clock when Timothy Rush, once the counsel of Martha and Mary College, now the lawyer who looked after the endowment that sustained the house on Walton Street, showed up on their doorstep. Kim was in the study reading to a preoccupied Emtee Dempsey a draft of her seminar paper when Joyce let the lawyer in.

Rush, his white hair in ringlets on his head, impeccably dressed in a chalk-stripe suit and navy blue tie, bade Sister Mary Teresa his usual respectful hello and, when Kim rose to leave the two of them alone, turned and looked at her over his glasses.

"Could you stay, Sister? My visit concerns you."

"Would you care for coffee?" Emtee Dempsey asked when Rush was settled in the chair opposite her desk. She assumed that everyone else wished to indulge in the endless consumption of coffee now denied her. Rush shook his head.

"I've just come from lunch. I had a somewhat difficult conversation with a lawyer named Sondergaard. WXYZ is a client of his."

"Oh," said Emtee Dempsey, getting comfortable in her chair.

"He told me the two of you have developed a sudden interest in the station's programming. Did you visit WXYZ this morning, Sister Kimberly?"

Kim nodded and Emtee Dempsey said, "Why would he bother you with something as trivial as that?"

"I'm not sure."

"What reason did he give?"

Rush looked momentarily uncomfortable. "He spoke of a ruse you were engaged in. He was remarkably well informed on your career and wanted to know what a medievalist of your stature would care about the programs on WXYZ. Of course I had no idea what he was talking about and I had to deal with his version of what had happened."

"I would like to hear that version."

It is remarkable how a single set of facts permits a variety of conflicting interpretations of their significance. Kim's visit to WXYZ, her interview with Bud Drabble, the intervention of Shearing when Drabble asked for the records of telephone calls made to "Air Affair," Shearing's promise to consult with Whitney and Sondergaard, were simply what had happened. But Sondergaard, armed with full information of Sister Mary Teresa's career, more than Drabble could have gleaned from the entry in *Who's Who*, more than Shearing had had, did not for a minute believe the story that "Air Affair" provided a possible parallel to events in the twelfth century.

"That does sound far-fetched," Rush said.

"It is."

"Why then did Sister Kimberly go there?"

"A far more interesting question is their reaction to her visit. Why is everyone but Mr. Drabble so nervous about curiosity in a public broadcast?"

"There has been dissension at WXYZ over the propriety of 'Air Affair.'"

"That is a story flimsier than my own. WXYZ is a business, is it not? 'Air Affair,' I gather, has increased their revenues. Drabble seems to think it rescued the station from a downhill slide. If this is true, I can understand why the upper echelon at the station overruled the attorney. They, after all, are businessmen."

Timothy Rush smiled slightly. "The same thought occurred to me. Sondergaard spoke of 'Air Affair' as of a guilty secret."

"As well he might. But in what does the guilt consist?"

"Have you listened to the program, Sister?"

"I know what it is. It is tasteless and exploitative. It is enough to make one weep."

"Well, then."

"I do not think it is an aesthetic judgment of 'Air Affair' that explains this overreaction to Sister Kimberly's innocent call on them."

"Innocent?"

"Perfectly innocent. My story is flimsy, I grant you that. The possibility that I could weave into my narrative of courtly love a reference to 'Air Affair' is remote indeed. But it is not through and through impossible."

"Just a story? What is your real interest in that program?"

Emtee Dempsey told him. After all, Timothy Rush was their lawyer as well as an old friend. Rush had taken a silver fountain pen from his pocket and, elbows propped on the arms of his chair, held it delicately at either end with his long-fingered hands. His manner was judicious as he listened to the tale of Enid Flaherty, of Kim's first hearing of "Air Affair" in the kitchen with Joyce, of Enid's murder and then Terry Stansky's. The discovery of the name Victor Sansfil in the two visiting books furrowed his brow until the old nun told him their interpretation of it. The story of Donald Schneider had been fed into the narrative as well and, when Emtee Dempsey had finished, Rush said, "If I were the police, I would follow the Donald Schneider lead."

"And you could well be right."

"The station has no obligation to show you its records."

"Doesn't your keen legal mind see some way I can gain access to them?"

Rush smiled away the compliment. "Yes. I can put the matter to Sondergaard without a misleading story to explain why the records are important. The simple truth is far more persuasive than your suggestion of historical parallels. Of course he will still refuse."

"Why?"

"Reasons would have to be given why he should give the records to you, not why he should refuse."

"But there is a strong possibility those records may be important in solving the murders of Enid Flaherty and Terry Stansky."

"All the more reason why he would be reluctant to turn them over to you. If your speculation is true, the records should go to the police."

"The police." Sister Mary Teresa made a face.

"An enormous amount of tax money goes toward the maintenance of a Chicago police force, Sister. Why not let them earn their money? It is not your job to solve the city's murders."

"Those women were guests in this house. Enid's son is staying with us now. I am not an outsider in this matter."

"I did not say you had no special interest in seeing justice done. But you are not an instrument of justice."

An old disagreement, however mild, threatened to be

rehearsed. It was a version of Richard's annoyance with Emtee Dempsey, although Timothy Rush was not as negative about the old nun's rushing in where only cops were meant to tread. Kim suspected Rush admired the way Emtee Dempsey's fertile mind often hit upon ideas that, however implausible they initially seemed, had a way of leading on to the solution of a crime that had baffled the police. Richard and his colleagues could scarcely be expected to be overjoyed by such amateur assistance, particularly when it was helpful.

Timothy Rush rose to his feet. "I'll let you know when and if I hear from Sondergaard again. But I doubt they will want to contact me."

"What are they hiding?" Emtee Dempsey mused.

Timothy Rush grew serious. "There is no indication they are hiding anything. They are, as you pointed out, businessmen. Businessmen are never eager to divulge their secrets."

"I don't want to look at their financial records. I want to see who made telephone calls to 'Air Affair.'"

"Don't count on it."

If Emtee Dempsey did not count on it, she certainly brooded about it. She had an extremely long telephone conversation with Katherine Senski in which, apparently, she tried to interest her old ally in yet another battle, but without success. Katherine could not be convinced that, even with the massive moral authority of the First Amendment in the shape of the *Chicago Tribune*, she could, under guise of doing a story on it, pry the telephone records of "Air Affair" from WXYZ. Kim, who had come into the study to consult a volume of Migne's *Patrology* and not been shooed out, stood with her back to Emtee Dempsey, holding the open book and following the conversation on the phone.

"Whatever happened to investigative reporting?" Emtee asked querulously.

The double-columned page she looked at was not the object of Kim's attention. She could imagine Katherine bristling at the implied criticism in Sister Mary Teresa's question.

"Think of the Pentagon Papers, Katherine."

Kim could not repress a smile. Did Emtee Dempsey imagine they could importune an employee of the station to smuggle out a copy of those records? The old nun's parallels were a bit exalted. Tragic as the murders of Enid and Terry were, it was difficult to see them on a par with issues of national foreign policy. Besides, Emtee Dempsey's approach was disingenuous. She had not been at all delighted when secret documents had found their way into the pages of the *New York Times*. She even developed a little homily on the restrictions on the people's right to know. She and Katherine had quite a heated argument about what Emtee saw as the press's tendency to portray itself as an unelected arm of government having the sanction of the Constitution itself. It was a mark of her desire to see the records of "Air Affair" that she should adopt Katherine's position while Katherine, apparently, fell back on Emtee's more modest notion of freedom of the press.

Having made no headway with Katherine, Sister Mary Teresa went back to brooding at her desk, working only intermittently on her manuscript. She was preoccupied at meals, even at dinner when Audrey also was with them. Meanwhile, Harry Flaherty still languished in jail, the police not accepting what to Emtee Dempsey was now axiomatic: he had not killed Enid. She was willing to concede that he had been involved in an altercation with Enid and her companion in the Tara Beer Hall on the fateful night, but she refused to see any further significance in the event. Harry's handkerchief in the death car? All she need do is postulate that the one who actually drove the car had seen fit to implicate Enid's husband by stuffing one of Harry's handkerchiefs between the front seats. It had been neatly folded, fresh from the laundry — Springfresh, as it happened.

Harry had retained Enid's habit, after leaving her, of having his laundry done at one of the many outlets of Springfresh in the city.

"How many are there?" Audrey pondered Emtee Dempsey's question. "I'm not sure. Dozens."

Joyce thought it remarkable that Harry had patronized his brother's establishments, given his animosity, but Emtee Dempsey dismissed this. The old nun seemed desperate indeed as she sketched various scenarios to explain how the handkerchief had been obtained. The manager, Hennessy, could have taken it from Harry's pocket when he roughhoused him out of the bar. Or Harry could have left it on the table where Enid sat with her unidentified companion the last night of her life.

"Making him the murderer," Audrey said, excited.

"Or you could have given the handkerchief to the man, Ms. Larson."

Audrey's mouth fell open and stayed open as Sister Mary Teresa went on.

"You work at a Springfresh outlet. Enid brought her laundry there. I assume it is possible that some of Harry's clothing had been left behind when he moved out of the apartment — among other things, handkerchiefs. Very well, you took one of them from her pile of clothes and..."

"I did not! What an awful thing to say. I did no such thing."

"I am just exploring possibilities, my dear," Emtee Dempsey said sweetly. "I don't suggest you actually were an accomplice."

Audrey got up from her chair. "I am not going to stay here a minute longer. It was stupid to come here in the first place. Come on, Marge."

It took all that Joyce and Kim and Marge could do to convince Audrey that Sister Mary Teresa was simply woolgathering. Audrey eventually sat down to finish her meal. Emtee Dempsey had lost interest in the commotion she had created.

From that time on Audrey and Marge were wary around the old nun. That night, when Kim was working in her room, there was a knock on her door and Audrey came in. She sat on the bed and looked anxiously at Kim, who turned her desk chair to face her caller.

"Sister Kimberly, does she really think I could do that with Harry's handkerchief?"

"She was only speculating."

"Are you sure?"

"Audrey, neither Sister Mary Teresa nor anyone else has any reason to suspect you of that."

"Not even you? I told you things, about Harry and me. You know I could have gotten hold of his handkerchief if I wanted to."

"And slipped away in the wee hours of the morning to put it in the car you knew would be used to kill Enid? Nonsense."

"But what if I did it accidentally? I mean, what if I gave Harry's handkerchief to someone, not knowing that . . ." Audrey bit her lower lip and tears welled in her eyes.

"Is that possible?"

"I don't know! That's what so awful. After she said those things, I can't say it's impossible."

"It's not very likely, is it?"

"I certainly didn't do anything like what you said the night Enid was killed. But I did have one of Harry's handkerchiefs. When I had lunch with him that time, I spilled some iced tea on my skirt and the place we were eating had paper napkins so he gave me his handkerchief. I dipped it in my glass of water and after I had taken care of my skirt, I put the handkerchief in my purse, telling him I would wash it for him." She smiled a miserable smile. "It was a way of seeing him again."

"Do you still have it?"

Audrey shook her head. "I thought of it that night, when he was at my place, and I couldn't find it."

"Where could it have gone?"

"I don't know."

A week had intervened since the lunch with Harry and the night he stayed with Audrey, the night Enid was killed. During that time Audrey had carried the washed and ironed handkerchief in her purse and she had been many places, with many people. Kim told her not to worry about it.

"No one could have known I had it, Kim."

"They couldn't know it was Harry's anyway, could they?"

Audrey looked worried. "His name was on it. Sewed on. Like a kid at school."

"Even so."

Kim assured Audrey again that all this was the craziest of coincidences, but when she was alone she wondered if Emtee Dempsey had stumbled onto something by letting her mind rove among possibilities.

None of this seemed to matter the following day when Freddy was kidnaped.

Eight

"Freddy's gone!" Joyce cried, rushing into the study. "He's not in the yard."

Joyce in her excitement still held the cigarette she had stepped outside to smoke. That was when she discovered that Freddy was not in the backyard where he had gone to play.

"He's been kidnaped!" Joyce crumpled into a chair.

"Put out that cigarette and compose yourself," Emtee Dempsey commanded. "When did you last see the boy?"

Kim got up and took the cigarette from Joyce and went down the hall to the kitchen with it. She took it out back, where she dropped it and stepped on it. The backyard was indeed empty. The entire area was bordered by a fence and at the rear of the yard a row of massive lilac bushes formed a screen concealing the alley. The gate was closed but they never locked it. Kim walked back to the gate and looked over it into the alley. It was a paved and now deserted alley, a narrow passage between the garages that abutted on it. Trash cans, like their own, were set beside the small aprons leading to the entrances of garages. Anyone could have come along the alley, parked behind their house, and entered the yard. If Joyce's fear was founded. But Freddy could equally well have gone through the gate and wandered away.

Kim went through the gate and, standing in the middle of the alley, looked first one way and then the other, undecided in which direction to go. In the end she walked down both, from time to time calling Freddy's name, her anxious voice sounding silly and ineffectual to herself. By the time she returned to the house she was inclined to accept Joyce's explanation. She had seen no sign of Freddy.

Emtee Dempsey looked at Kim when she came back.

"No sign of him, Sister."

"Where is Marge?"

"She's at Springfresh with Audrey, to keep her company." Joyce, still crying, answered as if Emtee Dempsey were accusing her of something. The old nun picked up the phone. Holding it, she asked Kim for Richard's number.

"I'll do it. He may be at home."

Emtee Dempsey hesitated. "What if the boy too is at Springfresh?"

"He can't be. How could he find it? He's only four years old."

"There's no chance they took him with them?"

"No!"

Sister Mary Teresa was simply clearing away obstacles to her anger. Two of the women who had come to the house on Walton Street had been murdered. Now the surviving son of one of them had apparently been taken from the house. She was in no mood for diplomacy. She let Kim dial the number but she kept the receiver.

Listening to Emtee Dempsey talk with Richard, Kim could imagine how her brother would take the veiled suggestion that the police were somehow in the wrong on this matter. How Richard and the Chicago Police Department could be held responsible for Freddy's disappearance it would have been difficult to say. Perhaps Emtee Dempsey simply wanted to put Richard on the defensive. It was always easier to deal with policemen when they felt vaguely derelict in their duties.

Richard arrived with Nealy and Horst in tow. He listened to Joyce while the other two went outside as Kim had done, to see what they could see. The tack Richard took was that he was confronted with three hysterical women. That the boy was gone was true enough, but that he had been kidnaped was fantastic.

"Why?" he demanded.

"You might as well ask why his mother was killed."

"She had a jealous husband," Richard said quietly.

"Perhaps she did. But he did not kill her."

Richard controlled his patience. "Okay. Imagine someone else did. What has that got to do with the kid?"

"That is what you must find out."

When Nealy came in, Richard made a phone call and soon the neighborhood was being combed by half a dozen uniformed police seeking a clue to Freddy's disappearance. The operating assumption was that they were dealing with a lost boy who would turn up within a block or two of the house on Walton Street, no worse for wear and doubtless a little surprised and frightened to be the object of a search.

Kim said, "Richard, the boy is four years old."

"I know about four-year-olds." Well, he had had several of his own, she couldn't contest that.

Despite his skepticism, before forty-five minutes had gone by, Richard switched to the hypothesis that Freddy's disappearance was a kidnaping. Emtee Dempsey accepted the concession in good grace.

"I would advise you to put through a call to Baraboo, Wisconsin," she said to Richard.

"Baraboo, Wisconsin?"

"It exists. It is the home of the Schneiders, Enid Flaherty's family. You will want to know if Freddy's Uncle Donald is there."

"I will? Why?"

"He has come here before and taken him away."

Richard was furious. "Why didn't you say that before? Do you mean the kid could be out with his uncle?"

"I mean that his uncle could be the kidnaper."

Richard looked at Kim but, receiving no comfort from her, made the call to Baraboo. Donald Schneider was nowhere to be found in that Wisconsin town.

Kim said, "The last time he was in Chicago, he stayed at the Holiday Inn."

Donald Schneider was not registered at the Holiday Inn. A check of Chicago hotels and motels was begun.

"What kind of car does he drive?"

It was Joyce who identified the family car as a Ford. But when Donald had taken Freddy to the aborted ballgame, he had been driving a Toyota pickup. Red. The latest model. Wisconsin plates. Richard notified the State Police.

"Okay," he said when that was done, "I'm going. Let us know if the kid shows up."

"He won't," Emtee Dempsey said and Joyce began again to cry.

When the Manila envelope was found in the mailbox of the house on Walton Street, there was no indication how it had arrived. There was no postage on it; for that matter, there was no address. It had been put there before the mailman came around, since it was his asking if he was meant to take it that alerted them to the envelope's presence.

"No postage, no address," the carried observed. He was a black with the physique of a football player rather than a mailman. He took off his cap and wiped his sweating forehead in the vee of his arm.

Kim held the envelope in both hands, studying it. "We didn't put it there," she said.

"Someone must have left it then."

Emtee Dempsey's reaction to the envelope exceeded her earlier flights of fancy. She laid it carefully on her desk and looked at it with a cocked eye. She might have been a robin studying a dubious worm.

"Open it," Kim urged.

"Sister, haven't you heard of letter bombs?"

"Oh, for heaven's sake."

Emtee Dempsey put out a pudgy finger and rotated the envelope on her desk. She picked up her letter opener but still hesitated with it poised before her. Kim felt like snatching the envelope and tearing it open but Emtee Dempsey's speculation gave her pause. Her mind told her that the thought of letter bombs was nonsense, but her nerves refused to be influenced by her thoughts. Emtee gingerly inserted the tip of her letter opener at the bottom of the envelope and then eased it in. When she began to cut through the heavy paper, Kim tensed as if an explosion would follow. It did not.

Emtee Dempsey cut completely across the bottom of the envelope, reached in, and pulled out several dozen photocopied pages. She glanced at them and a smile rearranged her face.

"Now, wasn't that thoughtful?"

"What are they?"

"I assume they are the telephone records of 'Air Affair.'"

When the old nun permitted her to see them, Kim was certain that is what they were. There were dates, the names of men and women who had been interviewed on the air, and the numbers of those who had called in to contact them. The records covered the time when the program began in late February and continued to April 24, the previous Friday. Kim found what she was looking for in the records for the last week in March. She showed it to Sister Mary Teresa.

"That is Enid Flaherty's phone number."

"The name is Wanda."

"Presumably all those names are false."

"Then there *is* a connection," Emtee Dempsey mused. She seemed almost surprised. But Kim thought, and said, that now they had the explanation of the station's odd reaction to their curiosity about these records.

"Who do you suppose sent them?"

"My guess is Bud Drabble."

"You mentioned Enid's name to him, did you not?"

"Yes."

"If he did send these copies, it may be that, since you were there, he made the discovery we have just made."

"But Whitney and Shearing and Sondergaard don't know?"

"It's possible. Katherine may be right. They had no obligation to show us these records. Their reaction could have been the normal secretiveness of the businessman."

"That isn't what you told Katherine."

Emtee Dempsey's acceptance of Katherine's explanation turned out to have an ulterior motive. This became clear when she called the *Tribune* and asked to speak to her old friend. Putting it as an hypothesis, she asked Katherine whether it would be difficult to identify callers simply by means of their telephone numbers. If not easy, it was certainly possible. Emtee Dempsey asked Katherine if she would come to Walton Street. It was an urgent matter. She smiled at the receiver.

"Yes, dear, I have them. They just showed up in our mailbox." A pause and a more expansive smile. "Cross my heart and hope to die."

Katherine came and was shown the photocopied pages as well as the envelope in which they had come.

"I still think you broke into the station and stole these."

It was not like Emtee Dempsey to deny too emphatically that she had done something outrageous.

"Now Katherine. Were the editors of the *New York Times* so skeptical when the Pentagon Papers were delivered to them? Don't look a gift horse in the mouth."

"I don't want to end up in jail."

"With luck, you'll avoid that."

Katherine went away with the photocopies, promising results as soon as she could obtain them. On Emtee Dempsey's urging, Kim put through a call to Bud Drabble.

"Thank you," she said.

"Don't mention it." He chuckled. "I mean that. Don't mention it. Unless of course something interesting turns up."

"Hasn't it already?"

"What do you mean?"

"Didn't you study them?"

"No. What have you found?"

"I'll let you know."

So much, apparently, for Emtee Dempsey's notion that Drabble had recognized Enid's telephone number in the March records and that this had prompted him to send the copies.

Donald Schneider was detained by the Wisconsin State Police just outside of Janesville. Freddy was in the cab of the pickup with him. Donald had avoided the Northern Illinois Tollway, going by US 12 and lesser roads, heading for Baraboo. The fact that he was in Wisconsin posed the prospect of extradition proceedings, so Richard dispatched Nealy to the scene. Donald's pointing out that he was Freddy's uncle made the Wisconsin troopers wonder if they had been enlisted in a pointless search, particularly when they learned that the boy's mother was dead and his father suspected of her murder. Where else was the kid supposed to be, if not with relatives? Dr. Michael Flaherty took somewhat the same line.

"Neither my brothers nor I have any wish to bring charges," he told the police. "This is a tempest in a teapot."

The publicity had died down and the Flaherty family did not want it stirred up again by the story that Harry's son had been kidnaped. It was pointed out to Dr. Flaherty that he was not the boy's legal guardian and in no position to waive charges. Besides, Harry Flaherty was furious. He had left his son in the custody of nuns and that is where he wanted him to stay. He sure as hell did not want the boy raised in the sticks of Wisconsin. Dr. Flaherty questioned whether a man under indictment was in a position to insist on his parental rights.

"Michael Flaherty was told that Harry certainly was," Richard said.

Emtee Dempsey, Kim, and Richard were in the living room. Richard was drinking the beer Joyce had brought him. She hurried back to the kitchen where, with Marge and Audrey, she was fussing over the returned Freddy. The boy had gone through the strange experiences of the past weeks with aplomb and was perfectly content to accept the attention he was getting from the three women.

"Our check on Donald Schneider's Chicago visits turned up lots of interesting things. So did his picture in the papers."

Both Hennessy and Jennie Probst recognized Donald as someone who had been in the Tara Beer Hall on a number of occasions. However, neither was willing to hazard a guess that it was Donald who was sharing a table with Enid on the night she was killed.

"Those letters suggest a motive," Richard said. "Nealy says the guy really sounded off his rocker up in Janesville. He was rescuing his nephew from the clutches of nuns, servants of the devil. God had instructed him to take the boy to Baraboo."

"How did the Almighty make himself known?" Emtee Dempsey asked.

"Search me. Mind you, I'm not saying Schneider wouldn't have a legitimate complaint about some nuns who shall be nameless. Now we're working on prints. So far it's all circumstantial. Schneider was in Chicago at the time of each murder. And there's motive. We'll need a hell of a lot more."

"You have as much as you do in the case of Harry Flaherty," Emtee Dempsey said. "Even more."

"Fine. A stand-off. Two suspects, not enough evidence. Aren't we lucky?"

"You may not be through yet."

"What do you mean?" Richard looked warily at Emtee Dempsey.

The old nun assumed a cherubic enigmatic smile. "Would you like some more beer?"

Richard, his euphoria disturbed by Sister Mary Teresa's remark, shook his head. He drained his glass and stood.

"Don't leave town," he said to Emtee Dempsey.

"I will do anything I please."

"Never kid a kidder. Don't bother, Kim. I can find my way out."

For the rest of the evening Sister Mary Teresa amused at least herself by sketching an elaborate story to cover the murder of Enid Flaherty. Why, it was quite simple when you thought of it. A man who had been seen around the Tara Beer Hall, with its reputation, was a man who would very likely rise to the bait of "Air Affair." Now, imagine the shock when the woman he contacts as Wanda agrees to meet him and he then discovers it is his sister. There is no fury like that arising from a combination of concupiscence and religious fanaticism, the old nun opined, and she gave several historical instances to illustrate the point. Donald, come to the assignation out of the promptings of the flesh, becomes as infurated as an Old Testament prophet when he discovers that his own sister has heeded those same promptings. Why, the thing had elements of Greek tragedy in it. His worst fears about the consequences of her disastrous marriage are confirmed, but she is no longer merely a victim. Now she is a sinner in her own right. Something must be done about it. He steals a car, plants a handkerchief of his hated brother-in-law in it, and, when Enid emerges from the Tara Beer Hall, he is ready. He blinks the lights to capture her attention. She stands frozen in the street. He presses down on the accelerator and runs over her. No wonder he broke down at the burial. His were the tears of guilt, not of grief.

Emtee Dempsey built up this story with evident relish and before long Kim began to find it possible, then plausible, finally it seemed almost probable. Of course it was made of whole cloth, there was not a shred of evidence that this is what had happened. But it could have happened.

"I wish we had those records here," Emtee Dempsey said. "Do you suppose we would find the number of the Holiday Inn?"

The records revealed something far more startling. Katherine Senski came to the house the following morning at eleven o'clock. The tall woman with the formidable hat looked sternly at Kim and marched down the hall to the study.

"Come along," she called over her shoulder.

Emtee Dempsey had heard Katherine's voice. Her fountain pen was capped and on the desk next to her neatly stacked manuscript. She sat with folded arms, a receptive expression on her round little face.

"We have hit the jackpot, Sisters. I will tell you what I have discovered and then we must notify the police immediately."

"What have you discovered?"

"First, you must assure me the police will be told. Immediately."

"Told what, for goodness sake?"

"No matter. I will tell them myself if it comes to that. No wonder the people at WXYZ are so skittish. Now they will have to explain why, knowing what they must have known, they did not inform the police."

"Katherine, you are a rival of the Delphic Oracle. Will you please tell me what those records reveal?"

What they revealed was not only that Enid Flaherty's telephone number figured in "Air Affair" but also those of a number of women whose bodies had been found in Cook County during the past several months.

"Dear God," Emtee Dempsey said.

"This is now completely out of our hands," Katherine said. "Notify the police, Sister."

"Sister Kimberly will take these materials to her brother. Your name need not be mentioned, Katherine. Unless you would like the police to know your part in this."

"Good grief, no. Keep me out of it. I'm satisfied that I will scoop everyone else. NUNS FIND 'AIR AFFAIR' LINK TO SLAYINGS."

"Katherine," Emtee Dempsey chided. But she could not help looking pleased.

Richard, in shirt-sleeves, hair rumpled, stood behind his desk talking on the phone. His expression was not welcoming when Kim came in. He nodded her to a chair and said into the phone, "Did you get an identification? How do you spell that? P-r-o-b-s-t. Probst, Jennifer. Cause of death strangulation. Find out all you can about her."

Richard hung up and scowled at Kim.

She said, "What has happened to Jennie Probst?"

"Do you know her?"

"She's a waitress at the Tara Beer Hall."

"Was. I thought the name sounded familiar. We interviewed her on the Flaherty case."

"She has been killed?"

"You heard me. Strangled. Her body was discovered this morning in the weeds beside the parking lot of Bradbury Chemicals. It looks like she was dumped there last night."

Kim remembered the story Emtee Dempsey had been weaving the night before, a crazy tale about Donald Schneider, putting him at the table in the Tara Beer Hall with Enid when Harry came in and they argued. Whoever that man had been, he had been waited on by Jennie. Did he fear she might be able to identify him? There was no reason for him to be fearful of that if he was not already implicated in Enid's death. Enid had left the bar alone. Had her companion preceded her outside? Had she been waiting for the signal of blinking headlights and stepped into the street only to be run down? What did it all have to do with "Air Affair?" Kim placed the Manila envelope on Richard's desk.

"What's that?"

He pulled the envelope toward him, sat and opened it. He leafed through the pages, telephone numbers beside which were now written names and addresses. Richard looked at her.

"It will take a while to explain, Richard."

"For God's sake, Kim. I'm busy. I don't have time to..."

"You have time for this."

Richard looked at the papers before him. She made the story as brief as she could, resisting the impulse to give it pace and drama as Emtee Dempsey would have done.

"How did you get hold of these records?"

"They were given to us."

"By whom?"

"They just showed up in our mailbox."

"Drabble?"

"Well, it had to be someone at the station. Whoever sent them, sent them anonymously."

"And you just phoned all these numbers and got the right names and addresses."

"We had some help there."

"I'll bet you did."

"Richard, this is the key to the killing of all those women."

"I don't see the Probst woman's name here."

"But she worked at the Tara Beer Hall. She saw the man Enid was with when Harry came in and started a quarrel."

"So what?"

"If he was the murderer..."

Richard made a face and gave Kim a little lecture. They would interrogate every person on these records. It would take time. They were not in the business of making wild guesses. Routine. Painstaking careful investigation. That was the way to handle a problem like this. Emtee Dempsey and Kim seemed to think that you sat down in a convent parlor and let your imagination roam. Well, that was okay for them. In fact, that is all he wanted them to do. He did not want any more interference, no matter how well-meaning.

"Richard, you would never have made the connection with 'Air Affair.' Can't you at least admit that?"

"Certainly not. Sooner or later it would have come out."

"Later. It's already too late for Jennie Probst."

"Thanks a lot. Another thing, Kim. Keep quiet about this." He dropped the photocopies on the desk. "I don't want to pick up a paper and read all about WXYZ and 'Air Affair,' understand?"

"We can't control that."

Richard groaned. "Meaning it's already known. Katherine Senski?"

"She was the one who found the names and addresses for all those telephone numbers."

"I'll talk to her. Not that it will do any good. If she writes this up, anyone responsible for those killings is going to be very difficult to locate."

"But you'll know who you're looking for."

"We will know the name of someone who has disappeared," he corrected.

"And the reason why."

"You haven't understood a word I've told you."

His phone rang and he answered it. He handed it to Kim. It was Joyce.

"WXYZ called. There have been several responses to your appearance on 'Air Affair.'"

"Joyce, stop it."

"Okay. Seriously. They want you to call."

"Who does?"

"He didn't say."

"It's the noon hour."

"I know. I'm feeding Attila the nun and Katherine. But he just called. He sounded urgent."

"Okay."

"Should I save some lunch for you?"

Kim said she would get back to Walton Street as soon as she could. She put down the phone and got to her feet. Calling WXYZ on Richard's phone would be unwise, given the mood he was in, plus her own anger at his ingratitude.

"If you want to talk with Katherine Senski, she's having lunch with Sister Mary Teresa. Good-by."

"I'm glad you brought this stuff down, Kim."

"You conceal it pretty well."

"I'm on edge. Sorry. I'll call Katherine."

Going down in the elevator, Kim felt sympathy of a sort for Richard. The police had been getting a going-over in the Chicago newspapers about the string of unsolved slayings and the mayor, in her press conference, had indicated that she was prodding the police to find the killer. Or killers. She gave the impression that if she herself could devote ten or fifteen minutes to it she would wrap it up but, alas, other duties forced her to rely on the police.

Apart from that, the chance that Donald Schneider was the man had gone the same way as the case against Harry Flaherty. Harry had been in jail when Terry was killed and Donald was in the custody of the Wisconsin State Police when Jennie Probst was killed. Dr. Michael Flaherty was now taking the public line that his little brother should be released. There was no case against him at all. The threat of a suit for false arrest was implied. This besmirching of the Flaherty name was not to be tolerated.

No wonder Richard was edgy. All the more reason why he should have whooped and cheered when Kim presented him with a link between the killings and "Air Affair."

From a phone in the lobby, Kim dialed the number of WXYZ. A man answered.

"This is Kimberly Moriarity. I received a call..."

"Yes. Could you come by the studio, Sister? Bud Drabble wants to talk with you."

"Can't you just put him on?"

"He would prefer not to speak on the phone. You understand."

"Who is this?"

"Charles Zimmerman. Mr. Whitney's assistant."

Kim looked at her watch. It was 12:40. So much for lunch. She told Charles Zimmerman she would come by WXYZ on her way home to Walton Street.

After she parked her car and came into the lobby of the building that housed WXYZ, she found Charles Zimmerman waiting for her. The little man she had seen typing in an office across from Studio A smiled in greeting and immediately grew serious.

"Bud is waiting for us," he said, taking her arm and starting toward the street.

"Where?"

"He'd rather not be seen talking with you upstairs. For obvious reasons. And he doesn't trust the station phones. A restaurant is better."

This held the promise of lunch and Kim was willing enough to go with Charles Zimmerman. Ever since she had spoken with Joyce she had been feeling ravenously hungry.

"Lead on," she said merrily.

He led her up the street to a parking garage where he asked Kim to wait while he brought down his car.

"Can't we walk to the restaurant?"

He laughed. "Do you want to walk to the McCormack Inn?"

"Why there?"

Charles Zimmerman shrugged. "I guess Bud likes the place. This isn't a good neighborhood for restaurants."

"He doesn't have to go clear to McCormack Place to find decent food."

"You know Bud. Or maybe you don't. I'll be right down."

What a strange little man Charles Zimmerman was. Except for the baldness, he might have been an altar boy. He seemed to know that Bud Drabble had sent photocopies of the records of "Air Affair" to Walton Street and was visibly enjoying the conspiratorial aspects of it all. Kim was eager to tell Drabble what the records of the program revealed, although she could imagine how that would make him feel. The sooner he got rid of "Air Affair" the better. He would shortly be getting a kind of publicity for the feature he would not want. For all Kim knew, his job might be in danger. But he had to know about those records.

A car swept down the ramp with Charles Zimmerman at the wheel. Kim stepped out of the waiting room as Zimmerman came to a stop. He leaned across the seat and opened the passenger door. When she was settled in and the car started forward, she said, "I'll call home from the restaurant. I should tell them where I am."

"Them?"

She told him briefly of the house on Walton Street where she lived with Sisters Mary Teresa and Joyce.

"That's where Margaret Pollock and Audrey Larson have been staying, isn't it?"

"How did you know that?"

He smiled. "Who do you think put the Manila envelope in your mailbox?"

"You?"

He nodded, pleased with himself. He was heading toward the lake, out of sync with the traffic lights, so they moved from one corner to the next, the sign going red just before they reached the intersection. "When I called Walton Street they said you were at police headquarters. I gather you have discovered why Whitney and Shearing and Sondergaard are so jumpy about 'Air Affair.'"

"Then they did know?"

"Drabble didn't. That's why he wouldn't listen to them when they wanted him to drop it. He's right about it bringing in a lot of revenue. That was his argument for keeping it and they didn't give him their real one for wanting to drop it."

"They should have told the police."

"They've been trying to figure out a way to do that without getting a lot of bad publicity. Ad revenue or not, it is a vulgar program. It's a disgrace to WXYZ."

"It is awful," Kim agreed. "How long have you been there?"

Zimmerman's baldness made his age difficult to guess. He said he had gone to work at WXYZ right out of college and that didn't help.

"Four years ago," he added.

That put him in his twenties still, probably not much younger than Kim herself. If he had said he was forty she would have believed it. Now he looked like a man in his twenties.

"What does Mr. Drabble want to see me about?"

"I really don't know."

"Could he have figured out 'Air Affair''s connection with all those killings? I'll bet he's heard about Jennie Probst."

Zimmerman looked at her without comprehension. They were on Lake Shore Drive now, heading south.

"She was a waitress at the Tara Beer Hall."

"What about her?"

"She's been killed. Strangled. They found her body this morning."

Zimmerman looked grim. "Whitney and Sondergaard have run out of time. They should have known silence would only protect the killer. And encourage him to go on."

"Why would anyone do such dreadful things?"

Zimmerman drove in silence for half a minute. "Perhaps he disapproves of 'Air Affair.'"

Bud Drabble awaited them at a corner table. A cigarette smoldered in an ashtray although he was in the process of eating his lunch.

"You eaten, Sister?"

"No, I haven't."

He gestured for the waitress. Kim ordered a BLT and a glass of iced tea. Zimmerman ordered a diet plate, which seemed odd. If anything, he looked underweight.

"He also jogs." Drabble made a face. He himself was clearly not on a diet. He dragged on his cigarette. "Sister, Charles has told me something terrible about 'Air Affair.'"

"She already knows, Bud. And so do the police."

"Oh, my God." His dismay turned swiftly to anger. "They should have told me. They knew and they didn't tell me. It's their fault this has gone on. I had absolutely no idea, not until you came to see me. When you suggested a connection between the program and the Flaherty woman, I had a suspicion something was very wrong. That's why I got photocopies of those records to you. And after you left I remembered where I had heard of Sister Mary Teresa before. If she was interested in 'Air Affair,' something had to be wrong. But I was truly flabbergasted when Charles told me how closely connected 'Air Affair' is to a whole series of killings. How did the police find out?"

"I told them."

Drabble sipped his gin and tonic. "Good. Now it will really hit the fan for Whitney and Sondergaard. Shearing knew too, didn't he, Charles?"

"He knew."

"I am going to make it very clear they didn't tell me. They owe me that at least."

"You're still going to be hurt, Bud."

Kim's and Charles Zimmerman's food arrived and Bud Drabble watched them eat as if he were still hungry. He ordered another gin and tonic and sipped and smoked in silence. From time to time people passing the table said hello to him and his face quickly assumed the smile of a celebrity. It faded swiftly. What would this awful news about "Air Affair" do to his popularity?

"How do the police intend to proceed, Sister?"

"I gather they will systematically question everybody on those lists."

"And everybody at the station?"

"I don't know. I imagine."

"Isn't it a crime to withhold information about a crime?"

Kim said she did not know. She could not blame Drabble for feeling vindictive toward Whitney and Shearing and Sondergaard. Nor could she understand what they had hoped to gain by keeping such a thing secret.

Zimmerman said, "Oh, they hoped the killer would be caught and there would be no connecting of him with the station. Stupid."

"Stupid," Drabble repeated. "My God, when I think they let me go on putting women in contact with men any one of whom could have been a killer, I could wring their necks. I wonder if I shouldn't make a statement to the press right now, Charles."

"Not a bad idea." A bit of lettuce clung to Zimmerman's lower lip as he chewed meditatively. "Protect your rear."

Before Kim left the restaurant she put through a call to Walton Street and was surprised when Sister Mary Teresa answered.

"Sister Joyce is in the backyard with Freddy. She's reluctant to let the boy out of her sight even for a moment. How did you fare with Richard?"

Kim's report did not stress the ungrateful way in which Richard had received the records of "Air Affair," despite their significance.

"Will you be returning now?"

"I should be home in half an hour to forty-five minutes."

"Good. I want you here when Mr. Whitney and Mr. Sondergaard call on me."

"They're coming to see you?"

"That's right."

"They've known the truth all along, Sister, but they didn't tell Bud Drabble. Needless to say, he is furious."

"These two gentlemen are a bit angry themselves. Don't delay."

Nine

Clarence Whitney, the station manager of WXYZ, and Olaf Sondergaard, the station's counsel, sat in straight-back chairs across from Sister Mary Teresa who, as usual, was pulled up to her desk whose surface, as was not usual, did not contain the impressive pile of manuscript pages of her study of the twelfth century. Whitney, a thick-bodied man with wavy gray hair parted exactly in the middle, was gripping the arms of his chair when Kim came in, while Sondergaard, lean, blond, and fifty-ish, regarded his client with some concern.

"You had absolutely no right to have those records in your possession. You had no right to turn them over to the police. Have you any idea of the irreparable harm this will do to WXYZ? I assure you, madam, that I hold you responsible for this. Liable in the legal sense."

"Come in, Sister Kimberly," Emtee Dempsey said calmly. "You knew I was expecting these gentlemen. The excited, somewhat irrational man who just spoke is Mr. Clarence Whitney."

"Irrational? I am angry, madam, but I am not irrational."

"The correct way to address a nun of my order is Sister."

Sondergaard, oil upon the waters, said, "Sister, you will appreciate that Mr. Whitney is understandably upset by your unlawful possession of private papers . . ."

"I received them in a perfectly lawful way. Gentlemen, the young woman who has just entered is Sister Kimberly."

The two men nodded and Sondergaard half rose from his chair in greeting. That being done, Emtee Dempsey turned to Whitney.

"The law that should concern you, sir, is the prohibition of murder. And the laws that govern the concealment from the police of knowledge of a crime."

"Murder? Suppression of evidence?" Sondergaard essayed an unsuccessful chuckle. "Come now, Sister. We are here to inquire how you came into possession of records that are the property of WXYZ."

"And that I subsequently turned over to the police when it became clear they are relevant to a series of murders that have taken place in this city in recent months. But I am sure you gentlemen already knew that relevance and . . ."

Sondergaard, less smoothly, took umbrage at this. "Be careful, Sister. You are making a most serious statement and before witnesses."

"I am indeed. What is the true purpose of your visit?"

Sondergaard put his hand on Whitney's arm to prevent his client from engaging in another outburst and smiled patiently. "Precisely what we said at the outset. We wish to know how you came into possession of private papers of WXYZ."

"I found them in my mailbox."

"Ah. So they were sent to you. By whom?"

"I have no idea."

"Was it Bud Drabble?"

"I told you I have no idea. The envelope was not addressed and there was no note or letter inside."

"Do you have the envelope here?"

"No. The police have it. Mr. Sondergaard, I find it difficult to believe you countenanced this absurd visit by your client. His quarrel is not with me; it is with himself. Why did he withhold knowledge of a crime from the police?"

"Because he did not have knowledge of a crime."

"That is difficult to believe. I have reasons to think it is untrue." Emtee Dempsey's eyes flicked to Kim. "In any case, that is a matter between yourselves and the District Attorney. As you very well know. There is no way that what has been done can be undone. The police now have the telephone records of 'Air Affair' and they know that a number of women whose pathetic pleas were broadcast by WXYZ were subsequently murdered. I repeat: why have you come to me?"

"If what you say about those records is true, it is dreadful. But this is the first I or my client knew of it."

"Then your anger is mystifying."

"To be angry at learning that private papers have been stolen is scarcely mystifying."

"I stole nothing."

"You received stolen property."

"I emptied my mailbox. I am appalled that your concern is solely for your reputation as a business concern, a reputation that can hardly be high when you broadcast such atrocities as 'Air Affair.' Your concern should be for those foolish women who were lured into making a public display of their loneliness and ended by being murdered."

Sondergaard rose to his feet and, taking Whitney's elbow, urged him to his. "This is not the end of this affair," he said in a soft menacing voice.

"I hope it is the end of 'Air Affair.'"

"Come, Clarence, I think we should go."

And they did, stomping down the hallway and closing the front door with audible firmness behind them.

"Dr. Flaherty telephoned to thank me for my efforts in saving the good name of the Flaherty family," Emtee Dempsey said, thereby dismissing as unimportant the visit of the two men who had just left.

Katherine Senski's story about "Air Affair" had appeared in the latest edition of the *Tribune* and there was an unctuous account of the sleuthing sister from Walton Street who had revealed the connection between WXYZ's notorious program and the recent series of killings in Cook County.

"What did you tell Dr. Flaherty?"

"That he was welcome to that by-product of my efforts."

"Charles Zimmerman told me that Whitney, Shearing, and Sondergaard knew there was a connection between 'Air Affair' and those deaths."

"Who is Charles Zimmerman?"

"He works at WXYZ."

"In what capacity?"

"Several, apparently. He is a sort of assistant to Mr. Whitney. He writes scripts and does various odd jobs. And he says those three kept what they knew from Bud Drabble."

"Enabling that inane and dangerous program to continue. It angers me that their denial of such knowledge will probably be accepted for want of a way to prove the contrary. In saner times they would be flogged. Or hung."

The story of "Air Affair" was on the front pages during the next three days but the articles in the *Tribune*, which appeared under Katherine Senski's by-line, were far and away the most thorough and interesting. On the second day she had published the names and addresses of all those who had participated in the program. Obviously she had taken the precaution of making a copy of the copy of those records before returning them to Sister Mary Teresa. An official spokesman for the police deplored the publication of the names but the mayor, in a press conference, applauded it. However, she had always received laudatory treatment from Katherine Senski, who regarded her as the best mayor Chicago had had in decades.

The appearance of a fire-breathing evangelist on the list rivaled that of a prominent local politician's for attention in the press. For the most part those mentioned came forward voluntarily to deny any wrongdoing. This was unnecessary if the volunteer did not appear in the records of those weeks during which the women who had been killed telephoned "Air Affair," but of course those most eager to establish their innocence had contacted the station during those weeks. Suspicion was eventually focused on a man who had called the station to obtain the number of Betty Piedmonte, the first woman to be killed.

His name was McHugh, he had a police record that included rape and other sexual offenses, and he was unable to account for his actions at the probable time the Piedmonte woman was murdered. Kim studied the photograph of the man, weak chin, thin hair worn long, his expression an odd blend of belligerence and fear. He had been taken into custody and was being closely questioned by the police. The rivals of Katherine Senski's paper filled columns with interviews with acquaintances of McHugh, highlighting one with his parole officer. The day after his picture appeared Hennessy was quoted as saying the man had been a patron of the Tara Beer Hall, something McHugh denied. Dozens of his denials had been disproved and more and more it appeared that McHugh was the one who had killed Betty Piedmonte. He was soon arraigned and indicted.

Emtee Dempsey, who kept up on all this via newspaper and television, grew restless as the net tightened around McHugh.

"Did he have anything to do with the other women?" she grumbled. "Did he indeed kill Miss Piedmonte?"

"I only know what I read in the papers," Kim said.

"Precisely the difficulty. You are right." A smile came over Emtee Dempsey's face. "It has been some time since we entertained your brother and his lovely wife, Sister. We must have them for dinner. It is lonely here now without guests." Marge and Audrey had returned to their own homes and Freddy was spending a few days with Marge, to give Joyce a well-earned rest. Kim pointed this out.

"I will help in the kitchen myself," Emtee Dempsey said. "It will be no burden on Sister Joyce."

"No," Kim said. "I'll prepare the dinner."

The thought of Sister Mary Teresa in the kitchen was an unsettling one. Blessed Abigail Keineswegs wished her spiritual daughters to be adept in the household skills important for the women of her era, not only cooking but also needlework, but Emtee Dempsey was even less able to prepare an edible meal than to do petit-point. She refused defeat in these spheres, however, despite ineluctable evidence, and out of an exuberant sense of obedience made infrequent forays into Joyce's kitchen with results painful to recall.

"As you wish. Do you suppose they would be free tonight?"

"I'll see."

It was her sister-in-law Peg rather than Richard whom Kim telephoned to issue the invitation. Richard might smell a rat, but if he was confronted with the fait accompli of Peg's acceptance there was little he could do but come. Peg was overjoyed and accepted without consulting Richard.

"Sure we'll come. It seems ages since I've been out of the house. Of course I'll have to find a baby-sitter."

"Bring the kids along if you can't find one."

"You're kidding. I want a night off. If you don't hear

from me that means I've found a sitter and we'll be there. What time?"

"Seven."

Joyce, who had been offended by the suggestion that she was worn out from having Freddy as well as Marge and Audrey in the house, rose to the occasion with her usual culinary imagination and when she called them to table that night it was to a feast. Richard had been softened up with two rather strong drinks as they talked in the living room, Emtee Dempsey all but ignoring him and plying Peg with questions about the children. The wariness with which Richard had entered the house was long gone when they settled down at the table. Emtee Dempsey asked Richard to say grace and he did, swiftly, as if fearful he would forget the words, and then Joyce began to ladle out leek soup.

It was Richard who made the first allusion to the deaths of Enid and Terry. Emtee Dempsey shook her head vigorously.

"Now, now. No shop talk. You must be sick to death of thinking of those matters all day. This is a night to relax and give your mind a rest."

"Oh, come now, Sister. I know your curiosity. And, in this case, you have a right to be interested."

"My interest, such as it is, is fully assuaged by newspapers and television, Richard. Joyce, will you pass that platter to Richard? A man is fully capable of consuming two steaks. More wine, Richard?"

Kim exchanged a glance with Joyce. Emtee Dempsey was playing Richard like a fish. Before the night was out he would be insisting on bringing them up to date on the police investigation.

"Thank you, Sister," Peg said. "It's all I hear about. Don't misunderstand me, Richie. I'm perfectly willing to listen to the story of your day. But this is our night out and Sister Mary Teresa is right. You have to give your mind a rest from it." Peg pushed her bracelet up her arm and traced the line of her hair with the backs of her fingers.

"All right, all right." Richard shrugged and drank some wine.

Emtee Dempsey sailed into a disquisition on medieval food and they all listened in rapt attention as she held the table much as she had her classrooms of young women. She is really a remarkable woman, Kim thought. And a very shrewd one.

By the time they adjourned to the living room for coffee and, in Richard's case, brandy, Richard was determined to respond to all this hospitality by telling Emtee Dempsey how things stood in what the newspapers referred to as the "Air Affair Murders." He knew her interest in such things. Besides, where would they be if she had not sent over the records of that radio program?

"Once their importance was clear, there was only one thing to do. Turn them over to the police." Emtee Dempsey spoke in pious tones.

"It simplified our work, I can tell you that."

Simplified? Kim thought. It *did* his work for him, providing the names and addresses as well as the telephone numbers of the participants in "Air Affair." All that remained was to go systematically through the list and establish connections. As they had done in the case of McHugh.

"He is definitely the man?" Emtee Dempsey asked.

"It looks firm. We're trying to make it firmer. The prosecutor needs everything we can give him."

"Do you have proof he contacted the Piedmonte woman?"

"You saw the lists," Richard said.

"Did she die by strangulation?"

"The only one who didn't was Enid Flaherty." A frown flitted over his forehead. "That's why we still have Harry Flaherty in custody. A different M.O. suggests a different murderer."

Settling back, Richard ticked off the murders on his

fingertips. Betty Piedmonte, February 23, strangled, her body found in a ditch beside a county road west of the city. Jane Timmer, March 9, strangulation. March 23, Michele Mooney, strangled. April 7, Enid Flaherty, hit and run. April 13, Terry Stansky, strangulation. Richard added Jennie Probst as if in an afterthought.

"Enid does stand apart from the rest," Emtee Dempsey agreed. "You say you can connect your man McHugh with the Piedmonte woman only tenuously."

"Well, it's not yet cut-and-dried."

"What links them other than the records of 'Air Affair?'"

"He took her out. We have solid proof of that. McHugh admits it. He gave us leads as to where they went, who might have seen them together. And there is his record."

"When you made your little list you avoided mentioning that the victims were raped. Were you simply being delicate?"

"No." But something like a blush suffused Richard's face. "All the women had been with a man shortly before their deaths but rape does not seem to have been involved." His blush deepened as he finished the remark.

"All the women?" Kim asked. In the corner, where they had been carrying on a separate conversation, Peg and Joyce had stopped to attend Richard's tortured remark. At Kim's question, they went back to their own topic.

Richard nodded. "All but Enid Flaherty, that is. Another difference."

"Terry Stansky?"

"Yes."

Kim was startled. And shocked. Terry had been heartbroken at what had happened to Enid and became ashamed of the way she and the MOMSIES had lived. Had she so swiftly gone back to her old ways? Sometimes Kim felt she did not understand other women at all.

"She had known a man just prior to her death?" Emtee Dempsey's Biblical phrasing helped.

"That's right. And, as with the others, except Enid, there were no signs of a struggle or the usual things that suggest rape."

"So it could have been someone known to these women?"

"Maybe. Maybe not. These women were hungry for companionship. When they met a man you could say they knew him, but that doesn't mean they had known him before."

"Or even have met him before."

Richard nodded.

"So a pattern emerges. Lonely women with a somewhat elastic conscience seeking male companionship. 'Air Affair' provides an opportunity. They broadcast their availability, interested men contact them via the studio. And among those interested men is a killer. He wants more than the thrill of romance; he wants to murder them. Why?"

"You'll have to ask a psychiatrist that, Sister."

"I am not likely to ask a psychiatrist anything," Emtee Dempsey said with distaste. "What would you say prompted McHugh to strangle Betty Piedmonte?"

"I don't speculate about that sort of thing. The prosecutor can worry about motive."

"Had McHugh ever harmed a woman before?"

"He was convicted on a rape charge," Richard reminded her.

"And where was Mr. McHugh on March ninth when the Timmer woman was strangled?"

"He can't account for his whereabouts."

"Can you?"

"He says he was drunk. He's an alcoholic and when he says drunk he means drunk." Richard put down his brandy glass. "Two, three days of more or less constant drinking, wandering from bar to bar."

"Then it should be easy to follow his itinerary during so public a spectacle."

"Not given the bars he goes to. The longer he drinks,

the lower down the scale of bars he goes. That's the pattern. But we have only his word he was on a tear when Jane Timmer was strangled."

"Was each woman strangled in the same way?"

This was disingenuous. Newspaper accounts made it clear that in each case a nylon stocking had been the instrument of murder. Richard said so now.

"Did the stocking belong to the victim?"

Richard frowned. "We don't know. Probably not, if you assume the other one would be at the scene of the crime. If the victim had been wearing them."

"He might have used one and taken the other with him. To use on his next victim. Do any of the stockings match?"

Richard looked at Emtee Dempsey closely and picked up his brandy glass. "If they did, that would be a pretty important link between the murders."

"I should say so. I gather such matching has been established."

"I didn't say that."

"But you don't deny it. So that is your link. The stocking used to strangle Betty Piedmonte matches that used to strangle Jane Timmer. McHugh killed Betty Piedmonte, ergo et cetera. Is that the reasoning?"

"It is a factual connection, scientifically established," Richard said primly. "We haven't been playing intellectual chess or anything like that. A steady accumulation of facts, that's how you get an indictment and conviction."

"Is there the same connection between the stockings used to strangle Terry Stansky and Jennie Probst?"

Richard squirmed. Apparently he had told more than he had intended, but equally he knew that Emtee Dempsey would not let him change the subject now. He nodded reluctantly. "This is absolutely confidential, Sister. It is the rock-bottom base of our case."

"And a good solid base it is."

"So you see it is not just a guessing game."

"If you can link McHugh to one of those stockings."

"The circumstantial evidence is strong."

"And that would give you a factual connection, scientifically established, between the killings of Betty Piedmonte and Jane Timmer. Did McHugh get in contact with Jane Timmer through 'Air Affair'?"

"He didn't telephone the station, no."

Emtee Dempsey's brows rose above her round glasses. Richard went on. "There was no direct contact. There is the possibility of an indirect one. One of the men who got Jane Timmer's number from WXYZ did time with McHugh when he was in for the rape conviction."

"Another possible killer?"

Richard shook his head. "He was in the county jail when Jane Timmer was murdered. McHugh could have got her number from his friend."

"And then you link the murders of Terry Stansky and Jennie Probst scientifically on the basis of the stockings used. Can you link them to McHugh?"

"If we get a conviction on the Piedmonte murder, we will be happy. That's all we need." He cited several cases where multiple murders had been reduced, for purposes of prosecution, to a single victim. Emtee Dempsey allowed that sounded reasonable enough.

"Where was Mr. McHugh on March twenty-fourth when Enid Flaherty telephoned 'Air Affair'?"

"I've told you we still assume the Flaherty killing is different. She was not strangled, she and her husband had publicly quarreled before the hit and run, he was notoriously jealous, and he had discovered her with another man."

"Have you identified him yet?"

"No."

"Those are certainly differences. And there is another."

"What's that?"

"Enid was killed on Tuesday, April seventh. All the other murder dates fall on a Monday."

"You think that's significant?" Richard's tone was not quite sarcastic.

Emtee Dempsey smiled sweetly. "Who knows? I couldn't establish scientifically that it is." Her tone was not quite ironic.

Kim decided it was time to intervene before this pleasant evening renewed the old quarrel between Richard and Emtee Dempsey. Richard's contempt for armchair theories had too often before collided with Sister Mary Teresa's belief that he and his colleagues were so often lost in the trees of fact that they missed the forest. Kim asked if anyone wanted more coffee. Peg looked at her watch and let out a squeal.

"It's almost midnight! Richard, I promised the baby-sitter we'd be home early."

She was on her feet. Richard drained the last of his brandy and got up too, not all that steadily. Kim, mindful of their uncles who had the Irish weakness where alcohol was concerned, did not completely approve of the way Emtee Dempsey had prompted her brother into talkativeness. She was relieved when, as they said good-by at the door, Peg announced she would drive. Richard gave her the car keys without argument.

Emtee Dempsey had said good-by in the living room and when Joyce disappeared into the kitchen, Kim found the old nun still seated, a frown on her face.

"Well, you certainly pumped Richard dry."

"Perhaps. There is not much in the well."

Kim shook her head. Emtee Dempsey was impossible to please. Whether he had intended to or not, Richard had almost certainly told them everything there was to tell about the police investigation of the murders and it was difficult not to see that the routine procedures he praised had turned up an impressive array of facts, no matter his relative ingratitude for the "Air Affair" records. When Kim said as much, Emtee Dempsey shook her head slowly.

"Yes, they are proceeding methodically down the road they have chosen. But it is the wrong road."

"What do you mean?"

"It's as plain as can be. Unless, of course, one insists on separating Enid Flaherty from those other unfortunate women."

"Because she was killed on Tuesday and not Monday? Come, Sister."

Emtee Dempsey planted her cane firmly preparatory to rising. Kim took her elbow and helped her out of the chair.

"It is far past time for night prayers, Sister Kimberly. Have Sister Joyce join us in chapel."

It was a distracted and exasperated Sister Kimberly who knelt in the chapel with Emtee Dempsey and Joyce, reciting Compline. The old nun was perfectly capable of teasing her with remarks like that. The police are on the wrong road! How could she possibly know? It wasn't that Emtee Dempsey was malicious, but Richard was right. She did have the most annoying tendency to suggest she could sit here in the house on Walton Street and, with a minimum of information, solve a crime that had a fair fraction of the Chicago detective bureau working on it. Kim tried with mixed success to rid her mind of these thoughts and say her prayers.

Later, in bed, unable to fall immediately to sleep, she reviewed what they knew of the murders, trying to find what it was that made Sister Mary Teresa so sure Richard and his colleagues were on the wrong scent. "It's as plain as can be," Emtee Dempsey had said, her tone matter of fact. It was not plain to Kim. Not that she didn't agree it was willful to refuse to connect Enid's murder with the others. Terry's death was so obviously related to Enid's. But Richard did have reasons for considering Enid a special case — and it was not that she had been killed on Tuesday rather than Monday.

Besides, the police had in custody a man who could have killed Betty Piedmonte and very likely had. If Emtee Dempsey thought the police were on the wrong scent, she had to come up with another that would lead to a flesh-and-blood murderer. Kim was doubtful the old nun could do that. She certainly could not do so by sitting in her study on Walton Street weaving possible scenarios of murder.

The trouble was she had done precisely that on many occasions in the past, as Kim well knew. So did Richard. But past successes were one thing; this horrible string of murders was another. If anything, Emtee Dempsey knew a great deal less than the police. The only factual evidence she had laid eyes on were the photocopied records of "Air Affair," and they were now effectively in the public domain, having appeared in their relevant entirety in the *Tribune*. Did Emtee Dempsey see something in them the entire city of Chicago missed, including its police force? This was preposterous. But Kim thought wearily, drifting into sleep, it was also, alas, possible.

In the morning Emtee Dempsey showed little disposition to discuss the matter further. After Mass and breakfast, she retired on the dot of nine to her study and plunged into the twelfth century as if she had not suggested the night before that she knew the police were mistaken and it was plain as could be that another tack should be taken. Kim was glad to go off to Northwestern and her graduate-student carrel in the library to work on documentation for the seminar paper she was due to read to her extremely critical peers the following week. She did not return to Walton Street for lunch, contenting herself with a sandwich and glass of milk in the student union. If she thought of Emtee Dempsey at all it was of the old nun hard at work in her study in the house on Walton Street.

When Kim returned to the house at three-thirty, she

found that Sister Mary Teresa had passed a very different day than she had imagined.

"Phone calls. Visitors. One after the other. You wouldn't believe it, Kim. She's been a whirlwind of activity," Joyce told her.

"Who's been here?"

Katherine Senski had come in midmorning and stayed for less than half an hour. Olaf Sondergaard, summoned by Emtee Dempsey, came at eleven and stayed past the noon hour but had not been invited to lunch. A man named Hennessy had been the first visitor of the afternoon.

"The first?"

"The other two are still in with her."

"Who are they?"

"Bud Drabble and another man from WXYZ. Drabble is short and fat and smokes like a chimney."

"I know."

"He doesn't look at all the way he sounds."

Kim went down the hall and tapped on the closed door of the study. "I'm home."

"Come in, Sister Kimberly."

When she opened the door, Bud Drabble and Charles Zimmerman were on their feet, apparently preparing to leave. Drabble wore a worried expression and gave Kim the most perfunctory of greetings. Zimmerman, forcing a smile, came and took her hand.

Drabble said, "I'm going to get a lawyer. I should have done it a long time ago. A few days ago, anyway."

"Olaf Sondergaard will represent you," Zimmerman said. "This concerns the station and we work for the station."

"Sure he does. He would represent me all the way to Joliet."

"Now, Bud. Things aren't as bad as all that."

Things seemed to be bad enough for Bud Drabble. The

study was clogged with cigarette smoke, and the ashtray beside the chair he'd sat in contained the ends of what seemed a package of cigarettes.

"Sister Kimberly will show you out," Emtee Dempsey said.

The two men were silent as they went down the hall, Bud Drabble trailing puffs of smoke, but his expression was not that of the little engine that could. At the door, when Drabble continued trancelike toward the street, Charles Zimmerman turned to Kim with a sad expression.

"Poor Bud," he whispered, and then was gone.

Kim hurried back to the study where Sister Mary Teresa was emptying Drabble's ashtray into a wastebasket.

"Would you get a candle and light it, Sister? That man is a walking Vesuvius."

"Would you like the window open?"

"That would be wise."

Having brought and lit a candle and opened a window, Kim closed the study door and turned to Emtee Dempsey. "Are you going to tell me what that was all about? Bud Drabble looks worried sick."

"I'm trying to stir something up."

"Is it a secret?"

"Something obvious can scarcely be a secret. I've been pointing out to several poeple, Mr. Drabble and Mr. Zimmerman among them, that the telephone records of 'Air Affair' do not point in the direction we all at first assumed."

Kim sat. "Do you mean the murders aren't connected with that program? Then why is Bud Drabble so worried?"

"The records are not the clue we took them to be. The earlier assumption was that someone whose name appeared on the list was the murderer we seek."

"That's not so?"

"Certainly not. Surely you can see why. Think."

"Please, Sister. I'm sure I'd never guess."

"It is not a matter of guessing. It is what your brother might describe as a scientifically ascertainable fact. The key is Enid Flaherty."

"Her name is on the list."

"Yes, it is. But how does it figure there?"

"As someone who telephoned Bud Drabble at WXYZ in connection with 'Air Affair.'"

"Exactly. She called in. But, Sister Kimberly, she was not interviewed on the program."

"What difference does that make?"

"It makes the very considerable difference that only someone who had access to the records would know of the call she made. In short, it is clear as can be that the killer is someone employed at WXYZ."

"But Enid must have telephoned a man whose number she got from Drabble, some man who was interviewed on the program."

"But she did not telephone him. Richard was kind enough to check that out with the only man interviewed on the day she called WXYZ."

"Did you tell Richard your theory?"

"With that information, my dear, it is no longer a theory. Only someone who had access to those records could have connected Enid Flaherty with 'Air Affair.'"

"Surely you don't think..." Kim considered the pathetic man who had just left the house on Walton Street. Could Bud Drabble be responsible for the deaths of Enid and Terry and those other women? And Jennie Probst?

"He is an obvious suspect. Anyone working at that station or having access to those records is a suspect. The beauty of it is that it ties together all the murders. I doubt that Richard in his heart of lion's heart really believes the police could have connected McHugh to all these women. His connection with the death of Betty Piedmonte is tenuous at best. Richard himself characterized the evidence as circumstantial. Not negligible, certainly, but undeniably circumstantial. It is logically possible that McHugh strangled Betty Piedmonte. But we know now that he did not. The fact that the killer is an insider at WXYZ removes in one fell swoop the difficulty of connecting one killer to all those women."

"Do you think Bud Drabble is a killer?"

"I doubt it in the extreme."

"Then who?"

"I have no idea. But the number of possibilities is limited. It is simply a matter of reducing the field to one."

"Well, that is something for the police to do. You should have told Richard all this."

"Sister Kimberly, he has all the information I have and more. It is difficult to believe he will not see what I have seen. Particularly when he now knows that Enid Flaherty did not make use of the phone number she obtained from Bud Drabble." Sister Mary Teresa sat back and steepled her fat little fingers. "I am happy to know that, while Enid might have been momentarily tempted by that silly program, she decided against contacting the man whose interview excited her interest. She was not without flaw, perhaps, but she had a residual sense of propriety." She put her hands flat on the desktop. "All the more reason to lament that her ultimate good sense did not protect her from the danger she ran in making that phone call to WXYZ. Her number was recorded, she had become the prey of a killer. I intend to expose him and have the satisfaction of seeing that justice is done."

"How will you go about doing that? Joyce tells me Mr. Sondergaard was here. Will you invite them over one by one and try to surprise the guilty party into a confession?"

"No. I have asked them all to come together. They will be here at eight o'clock this evening."

"They agreed to come here?"

"Mr. Sondergaard has assured me he will bring them all. Once I had pointed out to him that only someone who had access to the telephone records of 'Air Affair' could be the murderer, he proved to be quite amenable."

"Then why did you ask Bud Drabble separately?"

Emtee Dempsey smiled slightly. "Something you told me of your lunch with him suggested that might be advisable."

"Will he be here tonight?"

"Of course."

"When you expose the murderer."

Emtee Dempsey made a little bow.

"Sister Mary Teresa, you are playing with fire. If you are right, one of the people who will come tonight has already killed six women. The police should be here too."

"I couldn't agree more. I shall rely on you to invite them. I mean Richard, of course. It is only fitting he should take the culprit into custody when I expose him."

"Do you know who it is?"

"No. But I shall before the night is out. Would you telephone Richard?"

Kim called Richard and asked him to come to the house on Walton Street that night at eight o'clock.

"Kim, for the love of God, I'm up to my ears in a murder investigation."

"All the more reason why you should come. All the suspects will be here. Sister Mary Teresa plans to name the murderer and deliver him into your hands."

Even a nun of the new observance seldom hears the kind of language that Kim cut off by returning the phone to its cradle.

Ten

Katherine Senski arrived early, hung her wide-brimmed hat in the hall and examined her blue-gray hair, which, as usual, was braided and arranged in a coil atop her head. She turned from the mirror.

"Perhaps they'll all think I'm just another nun."

Kim laughed. "You would never have been just another nun, Katherine. Besides, everyone knows who you are."

Katherine tried to frown away her pleasure and, when she could not, stomped into the kitchen where Joyce and Marge were getting things ready for whatever orders their guests might have. Freddy was with Audrey in the basement apartment once occupied by hired help. She and Marge had used the apartment during their stay in Walton Street.

The three executives of WXYZ arrived at five minutes

of eight, standing on the doorstep for all the world like See No Evil, Hear No Evil, and Speak No Evil. Whitney was bracketed by Sondergaard and Shearing, a simian trio, but which was Speak No Evil?

Kim led them into the living room where they broke up as if by prearrangement. Shearing took a seat in a corner of one of the two couches near the fireplace, while Whitney took an upholstered chair, lowering his upholstered body into it. He might have been signaling for help when he pulled a pipe from his pocket.

"Do you mind if I smoke, Sister?"

"Not at all. There's an ashtray on the table beside you."

Richard came, bringing Nealy with him. The arrival of the police detective captain brought a thoughtful look to Whitney's nut-brown face. Sondergaard, who had been pacing the room as if to establish its dimensions, paused and bowed to Richard. Shearing shook Richard's hand vigorously.

"Thank God you're here. That gives this get-together some semblance of being official."

"I'm only here as a guest," Richard growled.

"Don't you know what she plans to do?"

"Sure. She is going to name the murderer of six women." Richard smiled, but if he meant to be sardonic, he failed, or so at least Kim thought. Still and all, she wished she felt more confidence in Sister Mary Teresa's ability to do what she promised to do. The old nun was in her seventies, after all, and she had slowed down physically. But Kim had detected no diminution whatsoever of Emtee Dempsey's considerable mental powers. Quite the contrary. Yet it was inevitable that someday they would begin to wane. Kim prayed that tonight would not mark the beginning of Sister Mary Teresa's decline. To attempt a great coup before all these witnesses and fail . . . Kim shivered. Emtee Dempsey, typically, professed to be exhilarated by the challenge.

"Afraid?" she had asked at dinner. "Afraid of what? I doubt I run any risk of physical danger."

"But aren't you afraid you might fail?"

"You make it sound like a great feat, Sister Kimberly. I only wish the scholarly problems I face were so easily solved. It is a simple matter of elimination."

"You're that positive?"

"My dear child, you make too much of it. How is your seminar paper progressing? Did you make the revisions I suggested?"

There was no way in the world Kim could think of that paper when there would soon be eight guests in the house — not counting Freddy, Marge, and Audrey — one of whom, if the old nun was right, had murdered six women. And Emtee Dempsey proposed to point her finger at the killer. Seminar paper indeed!

"I hope you guess right," Joyce said.

"Guess?" Emtee Dempsey tried the word as if for taste and her brows rose. "I will accept that. But there is a logic of guessing, you know. Perhaps guessing is the general subject matter of logic."

And off she went, describing the pursuit of a conclusion from premises as a species of guessing. Consider too the random choice between two closed fists, one of which holds half a dollar. If the choice is repeated, probability enters in, as well as your knowledge of the tight-fisted person. Joyce groaned audibly and Marge listened with open mouth.

"Is she just making that up?" she whispered to Kim.

"Guess."

It might have been a sign of apprehension that Sister Mary Teresa remained in chapel when Kim and Joyce left, her fat little fingers moving slowly over the large beads of her rosary. Kim asked about that when Emtee emerged and was told the old nun had just remembered it was the anniversary of her cousin Bridget's death and she wanted to say some extra prayers for the repose of her soul.

"And for the souls of those poor murdered women." Her eyes sparked and it was clear that her intention to name the murderer was more than a logical game. Sister Mary Teresa took it as a religious obligation to hunger and thirst after justice and she had no patience with those who became sentimental on the subject of punishment. She had a little lecture on capital punishment to counter maudlin denials of the moral responsibility of the human agent.

Charles Zimmerman brought Bud Drabble at ten minutes past the hour when Sister Mary Teresa had already emerged from her study and taken a thronelike brocade chair that faced the fireplace. Zimmerman was neat as a pin, as usual, suit coat buttoned, tie straight, the remaining hair on the sides of his head brushed slickly back. By contrast, Bud Drabble was a rumpled mess and he seemed unsteady when he crossed the room. He bowed deeply to Sister Mary Teresa and Zimmerman grabbed his elbow as if fearful Drabble might continue forward and execute a somersault across the room. Drabble sank onto the couch across from Whitney as the men from WXYZ exchanged nervous distracted nods. Drabble looked around.

"No one's drinking. What is this, a dry county?"

Sister Mary Teresa smiled. "I thought we might get started first, Mr. Drabble. I have a few things to say and I am sure many of you will wish to comment. In due time refreshments will be served. You realize you are late?"

"Isn't 'tardy' a better word, Teacher?"

"Relax, Bud," Whitney advised. The station manager crossed his arms and, with more difficulty, his legs, and his smile was tolerant. He seemed to be indicating by his posture how he wanted the others to comport themselves.

Kim was to Emtee Dempsey's right, slightly behind her, in a straight-back chair. She had a good view of everyone as the scene for the great revelation was set, even of Nealy, who stood next to the door with his back against the wall. Sister Mary

Teresa faced the fireplace on whose mantle an ormolu clock indicated eight-twenty. On the couch to the left of the fireplace Whitney and Shearing were seated; Olaf Sondergaard, hands in his pockets, leaned against the mantle. Richard sat behind that couch, in a chair angled to face Emtee Dempsey. Bud Drabble and Charles Zimmerman were on the opposite couch, the latter sitting on the edge of the cushion, hands on his knees, a receptive expression on his face. Katherine Senski, who had come into the room after Emtee Dempsey, but before the arrival of Drabble and Zimmerman, sat behind the two latecomers.

"You have said you will name the person responsible for the deaths of six women," Olaf Sondergaard said. "That is a most provocative statement and it explains why were we willing to come here. Very well. Who is the killer?"

"That is not why you are here, Mr. Sondergaard," Sister Mary Teresa said, smiling, though there was reproof in her voice. "Not entirely, in any case. You are here because I told you that only someone who had access to the records of the feature called 'Air Affair' could be responsible for these dreadful murders. Since those records were closely guarded, the culprit must be an employee of WXYZ."

"Or someone who illegally gained possession of those records," Sondergaard said dryly.

"Has there been a break-in at the station?" Sister Mary Teresa asked, equally dryly.

"There has been a breach of security, yes. You yourself managed to obtain photocopies of the 'Air Affair' records. Who can say how many other copies might have been made?"

Whitney turned from Sondergaard to Emtee Dempsey to see how she would reply to that. Kim had the impression Sondergaard had just played a card he and the station manager considered a trump that would undermine any claim the killer had to be employed by WXYZ.

"Not good enough, Mr. Sondergaard. Did you perhaps have a copy of those records at your law office?"

"Certainly not."

"An X in algebra is only of value if we know at the least that there is an unknown quantity. Then its identity can be determined by other known values. Your supposition of other copies of those records floating around the city of Chicago will not do."

"Perhaps we should stop fencing and hear what we have come to hear," Whitney said. "Will you give us the name of the murderer?"

"Yes."

Whitney unfolded his arms and legs. Shearing leaned forward, Sondergaard pushed away from the mantle, and Bud Drabble shook his head as if to clear it.

"Well," Shearing said when the pause continued. "Who is it?"

"Victor Sansfil."

There was a confused silence broken by Olaf Sondergaard's joyless laugh. "My dear lady, if that is the best you can do, you have wasted our evening." He explained to Whitney that this name had appeared in the visitors' books of the funeral homes from which Enid Flaherty and Terry Stansky had been buried. To Emtee Dempsey he said, "That is merely an X of the kind you were just deploring."

"On the contrary. It is one whose value can be determined from other known things. It is, of course, a pen name. A *nom de guerre*. And a message. I need not tell you what Victor means. Sansfil, unlike the presumably Latin Christian name, is from the French. Without wire. Wireless. Telegram, but also radio. The mock mourner who is actually the murderer was taunting us with a clue. He was drawing attention to WXYZ. Thanks to Sister Kimberly, it was that name which drew my attention to Mr. Drabble's 'Air Affair.' When the telephone records of the program came into my hands..."

"Sent to you by the murderer?" Whitney asked.

"I sent them to her," Bud Drabble said and looked belligerently around.

"Is that a confession, Bud?" Sondergaard inquired.

"To sending the records, yes. I thought she was interested in helping some woman whose name was on the lists." He stopped and shook his head. "No. That's not it entirely. When Kimberly Moriarity came to talk with me, after we disposed of the cock-and-bull story about 'Air Affair' and the Middle Ages, Enid Flaherty's name was mentioned. Maybe something clicked before she came, when I read of that hit and run. Something sure as hell clicked when Sister Kimberly mentioned it to me in Studio A."

"So you unilaterally took it upon yourself to jeopardize the good name of WXYZ?" Sondergaard tried to look shocked.

"Oh, cut the crap, Olie. WXYZ may survive this, but what's going to happen to me?"

"You're going to lose your job," Whitney said quietly.

"Are you serious?"

Whitney nodded. "'Air Affair' was a dumb idea in the first place. I ought to fire myself for letting you go ahead with it."

"You liked the idea! You fought for it with Zip and Olie. They might have been against it, but you weren't."

"I should have taken counsel from counsel. But making your records available to . . ." Whitney looked at Sister Mary Teresa and let it go. "That was disloyal, Bud. Forget about your lapse of taste on 'Air Affair.' You betrayed the station."

Sister Mary Teresa rapped the arm of her chair with her knuckles, bringing them to order.

"You can have your falling-out somewhere else at another time. Perhaps you will be less interested in recriminations when we have achieved our purpose tonight. This might be a good time for the refreshments I promised you. Sister Kimberly, will you see what our guests would like to drink?"

Whitney wanted nothing. Shearing wondered if he could have gin and tonic. He could. Emtee Dempsey had instructed Joyce to be ready to serve a variety of drinks and Audrey had advised her on what they might need. Sondergaard asked for Scotch and water. Richard shook his head, and Nealy, reluctantly taking his cue, did the same. A Coke for Charles Zimmerman and another gin and tonic for Bud Drabble. Katherine wanted wine, chablis would be nice.

"I will have chablis as well," Emtee Dempsey said. She put her hand on Kim's arm. "Have Audrey help you serve."

Richard came into the kitchen with Kim and took a beer from the refrigerator. He poured a glass and drained it.

"She doesn't know a damned thing, does she?"

Joyce and Audrey, who was being spelled by Marge in the basement apartment with Freddy, took over the preparation of the drinks so Kim had no easy way to avoid Richard's question. For all of Emtee Dempsey's talk of the logic of guessing, there seemed more guessing than logic in what had gone on thus far. All her revelations were ones she had already made and it was difficult to see how she could advance beyond her conviction that one of the men from WXYZ was Victor Sansfil. Even if she could do that, where would she be? A ghoulish joke might have been perpetrated by one of them without linking him to the murders. That might have been a device to draw attention to someone else.

"We'll have to wait and see."

"I'm not going to wait too damned much longer." Richard poured out the rest of the beer and drank. Kim stopped him before he emptied the glass.

"Give me a sip."

He handed her the glass with a wry smile, as if she had just admitted doubting Sister Mary Teresa. Joyce and Audrey had gone into the living room with the drinks. Richard left and Kim went to the basement door. There was the murmur of television from below. Freddy was staying up late tonight. Marge really ought to take the boy upstairs to the guest room and put him to bed. Kim turned as Audrey came into the kitchen. There was an excited expression on her face.

"Tell her yes," she whispered. "I recognize him. The little fellow."

"Mr. Shearing!"

"Is that his real name? He called himself George."

"What about him?"

"Just tell Sister Mary Teresa I said yes," Audrey urged, her hand on Kim's elbow, steering her toward the living room.

The drinks had relaxed the visitors somewhat and there was the buzz of several conversations. Emtee Dempsey held her glass of unaccustomed wine by the stem and looked out over the gathering with a speculative eye. Kim bent down to speak to her.

"Audrey says yes."

Emtee Dempsey nodded, but there was no display of emotion. Kim was not sure what message she had brought.

"Very well," Emtee Dempsey said in a loud voice. "Perhaps we can return to the business before us. Is everyone satisfied with his drink?"

There were murmurs of satisfaction around the room and little indication that the seriousness of the occasion bothered anyone.

"We have established," Sister Mary Teresa went on, "that only someone who had access to the records of 'Air Affair' could have known about each of the women who met her death, in all but one case by strangulation. This means that an employee of WXYZ is the murderer." She lifted her hand to stop an objection from Olaf Sondergaard. "I am now prepared to identify that employee."

"Victor Sansfil," burbled Bud Drabble, dipping into his drink.

"Yes. Victor Sansfil." Emtee Dempsey paused and her eyes moved on from Bud Drabble. "And Victor Sansfil is Charles Zimmerman."

Shearing sputtered into his glass, a startled sound came from Whitney, and Richard crossed the room to get behind the couch on which Charles Zimmerman sat. But the most noticeable reaction to Sister Mary Teresa's remark was the trilling helpless laughter of Charles Zimmerman. It rose toward falsetto, then settled into a guttural expression of uncontrolled mirth. Sister Mary Teresa waited until the young man was through laughing.

"This is absurd," he said, his eyes filled with tears, and began to laugh again.

"Enough!" Emtee Dempsey barked with the authority of the long-time professor. Charles Zimmerman fell silent.

Olaf Sondergaard said, "Have you any proof to sustain your accusation?"

It may have remained a legal question to him, but both Whitney and Shearing were looking at their junior colleague with intensity and the beginnings of doubt. Bud Drabble seemed imperfectly aware of the significance of what had just been said.

"You wrote your taunting pen name in the visitors' books and, in the case of Enid Flaherty, you even had the contempt to attend the burial of the woman you had killed. It was there that Terry Stansky recognized you and thereby put her own life in danger. Despite the brazenness of your actions, you could not believe that anyone who recognized you in your ridiculous disguise would not make the inference that imperiled you. So you strangled Terry Stansky, resuming your usual *modus operandi*. The wig you wore will likely be found by the police where you live."

"Are you saying the witness against him is dead?" Sondergaard still acted as if this were a tactical exercise. "And what on earth did she witness?"

"Seeing Mr. Zimmerman at the cemetery prodded her memory and she realized it was Charles Zimmerman who was Enid's companion when her husband came into the Tara Beer

Hall and started the argument that led to his ejection. It also prompted a variation in your method. A hit-and-run killing would turn attention to the irate husband. But Charles Zimmerman was the last person to be with Enid Flaherty alive. Fortunately, there are other witnesses to Mr. Zimmerman's habits."

"Who?" Richard demanded.

"Sister Kimberly, will you ask Audrey Larson to come in here again."

As Kim started from the room, Charles Zimmerman revealed his desperation. He was on his feet and had started to move when Bud Drabble stuck out a foot and sent the young man sprawling across the floor. He landed at Sister Mary Teresa's feet. Immediately, Richard and Nealy descended upon him and subdued him. Upright, pinioned by the two detectives, he glared at the old nun with hatred. There was no trace of the scoffing laugher of a few minutes before.

"You should be grateful to me for what I did! That filthy program! Those depraved women. It was God's work to rid the world of them and I'm glad I did. They did not deserve to live."

"None of us does, Mr. Zimmerman," Sister Mary Teresa said calmly. "Life is a gift."

Zimmerman strained toward her, his eyes bulging, and nearly freed himself from his captors. But they pulled him back and got more secure holds on him.

"Let's go," Richard said and, with Nealy's help, he half led, half carried, the raving assassin from the room.

"Superb!" Katherine Senski said. "Absolutely superb. I must telephone the rewrite desk. Please excuse me." And, with a flourish, she swept out of the room and into Emtee Dempsey's study.

"My God," Whitney said. "I can't believe it."

"Charles," Shearing murmured. "Charles Zimmerman. He actually killed all those women?"

"You heard him," Emtee Dempsey said coldly.

"And what would you have done if he hadn't confessed?" Olaf Sondergaard asked, but his voice betrayed the wonder at what had just occurred. A man who had murdered six women had just been dragged from the room! Sondergaard walked to the couch and was about to sit where Zimmerman had sat and then thought better of it. He went on to the chair vacated by Katherine Senski. "Could you have proved it if Charles had denied his guilt?"

Sister Mary Teresa's smile was enigmatic. She brought her wine to her lips, sipped it delicately, then put the glass on a table beside her chair.

"I said I would name the murderer and I have done so. This should come as a great relief to WXYZ."

Those were Clarence Whitney's sentiments. He came to Sister Mary Teresa and took her hand in his.

"I, for one, am profoundly relieved. Oh, there will be some bad publicity in the short run, but nothing like what there would have been if the killer had not been found. You did have proof, didn't you?"

He received no direct answer to his question. Audrey Larson came into the room and looked about with a frightened expression on her face.

"He's gone, dear," Emtee Dempsey said. "You have nothing to be afraid of."

Bud Drabble, the nature of the outcome clear to him at last, lit a cigarette, exhaled smoke with a great sigh, and said, "Could I have another drink?"

They all had another drink, all but Sister Mary Teresa.

The party — for that is what it seemed now that the WXYZ personnel no longer felt under suspicion — went on for forty-five minutes more. Finally Whitney rose to go and again he took Sister Mary Teresa's hand.

"Thank you, Sister. I will not conceal the fact that I was very annoyed at your, well, curiosity about the station. Now

I am in your debt. We all are. A heavy cloud has been removed."

"You should have removed it yourself as soon as you discovered the connection between 'Air Affair' and the deaths of those women."

Olaf Sondergaard nervously intervened. "Unlike yourself, Sister, we were reluctant to move from guesses to accusation."

Sister Mary Teresa gave the lawyer a long look. "I can understand your reluctance but I refuse to accept your interpretation of it."

Sondergaard did not press the matter and soon, with the somewhat exuberant Bud Drabble in tow, Sondergaard, Whitney, and Shearing were on their way.

"Congratulations," Kim said when she came back from showing the visitors out. Katherine had finished phoning and was back in the living room.

"Sister Kimberly, will you ask that woman to come here. Audrey, isn't it?"

Kim received a nod from Emtee Dempsey. Audrey was not in the kitchen, but Kim found her in the basement apartment, talking with Joyce and Marge.

"Why don't you all come upstairs?"

"Are they still up there?"

"Just Sister Mary Teresa and Katherine Senski."

When the women were all settled in the living room, Katherine said, "Now then, Audrey, tell me how you recognized Charles Zimmerman."

"Oh, Katherine," Sister Mary Teresa sighed. "Can't you guess?"

"I would prefer an explanation."

"The Tara Beer Hall," Audrey said. "I had noticed him there several times. He didn't seem to belong. Yet he always seemed to be with someone when I saw him there. When Sister Mary Teresa showed me pictures of the women who had been killed I recognized one of them as a companion of his at the Tara. Sister asked me to serve drinks tonight and see if I could find that man in this room. And he was here." Audrey's eyes seemed dragged to the couch where Charles Zimmerman had been sitting.

"Sister," Katherine said, "you are lucky he blurted it all out the way he did."

"Nonsense. Conscience is a great ally in such matters, it is true. *Ayenbyte of inwyt.* Imagine the burden of guilt that man was carrying. But when Audrey recognized him, he recognized her. He knew he was doomed, as he would have been doomed if Terry Stansky had lived."

Sister Mary Teresa seemed no more impressed in subsequent days, when everything fell into place. A wig was found in Zimmerman's apartment, as well as nylon stockings he could not explain but that had been destined for the throats of women whose easy morals both attracted and enraged the twisted little man. Emtee Dempsey was impatient with suggestions that she knew nothing in Charles Zimmerman that would explain his vicious killing. "You can put that burden on those who worked and lived with him. Perhaps they might have suspected the depths of his emotions. More likely not. But that has nothing to do with me. He was an X and I had to proceed from what I could know." Richard was exuberant when Zimmerman's fingerprints matched some taken from Enid's and Terry's apartments. To him this was of far greater importance than the accumulating circumstantial evidence. Zimmerman could not account for his whereabouts at the times of any of the killings. He was bound over to the grand jury.

When Harry Flaherty came by for Freddy, their reunion was emotional and the three nuns suddenly realized how lonely the boy had been during his stay with them. Emtee Dempsey came to the door with Kim and Joyce and watched them go out to Harry's car.

"The prodigal father," she murmured.

The three of them went into the chapel then for Vespers, to recite the psalms of the hour, part of that great sorority of praying women who went back to the era of the Blessed Abigail Keineswegs and beyond, to the twelfth century, to the earliest times.